First Lady Down

Mary Jane Owen

Pepperback Press, Inc.

Copyright © 2025 by Michael Owens

All rights reserved.

No portion of this book may be reproduced in any form without written permission from the publisher or author, except as permitted by U.S. copyright law.

1

Friday Afternoon

I'm too old for this shit.

"With all due respect, Madame Former First Lady," Ambassador Al-Rashid gestured toward me with a wave of his hand as he continued stiltedly, "your assurances ring rather hollow given your current administration's positions on carbon emissions and pandemic preparedness." It had been a long damn week and everyone was at the end of their rope, but Al-Rashid was in particularly bad shape, his face pale and his eyes red.

I breathed in the bitter clouds of stale coffee and repressed hostility that floated toward the high, gilded ceiling of the ballroom and cast my gaze at the collection of political appointees that shifted restlessly around the U-shaped table, waiting for my response. Their faces hid boredom and annoyance with varying degrees of success.

Al-Rashid knew damn well that wasn't my title. I took a sip of water from the glass at my elbow, reaching deep down for my last ounce of diplomacy.

The water was warm.

Al-Rashid continued with a frown. "Perhaps your time would be better spent convincing your own government of the urgency of these crises, rather than lecturing the rest of us." He leaned back in his chair and crossed his arms as he stared down his hawkish nose at me.

The other delegates exchanged subtle glances as I forced myself to swallow the tepid liquid in my mouth.

That's it, I thought with a moment of perfect clarity. *That's the straw.*

"You're right," I said coolly, relaxing my eyebrows and letting my face settle into my natural expression. RBF, I believe the kids call it.

The room went quiet as murmured conversations came to an abrupt end.

"What can I say?" I asked, setting down my glass of warm piss with a click that echoed in the sudden silence. "The current President's position on climate policy is, to use the technical term, idiotic."

Someone at the back of the room made a choking sound.

Al-Rashid was staring at me blankly. "Excuse me?"

"I'm agreeing with you." I folded my hands on the table, my wedding ring catching the light. "We're all tired, Ambassador. But here's the thing—"

I leaned forward, holding his gaze as I crossed a bridge. And set it on fire.

"—he won't be in office forever. These problems can't be reduced to election cycles or political theater. We can sit here and score points off each other's domestic failures, or we can get off of our collective asses and do the work we came here to do."

Al-Rashid's jaw tightened, the muscles visible under the skin. "Madame Barrett—"

The lights flickered and went out.

Everyone froze for a long moment, but the room remained dark. Around the table, the other delegates began pushing back chairs and surging to their feet in a cacophony of shouted questions in half a dozen languages.

"*Restez assis!*" one of the French security officers barked. "Everyone remain seated!"

A hand clamped around my arm. The head of my Secret Service detail materialized at my elbow like he'd been conjured from thin air, which was basically his superpower. Henry's other hand was already on his sidearm, his body angled to put himself between me and the windows.

"Let's go," he said, his voice clipped and professional. "Now."

I sighed in resignation as he maneuvered me out of my seat. Two members of my security detail appeared beside us and soon I was sandwiched between them as we walked briskly toward the door.

"Hellcat on the move," he said into his wrist mic. "Heading for the secondary location."

I opened my mouth to argue and earned myself a side eye that could peel paint. Henry was absolutely not interested in my input on this particular topic at this particular time.

"So dramatic," I muttered under my breath.

The darkened hallway was controlled chaos, but Henry and I had played this game before. Our little group walked calmly past security personnel with flashlights, barking orders in French. Delegates from other sessions were being herded toward various exits, their faces ranging from annoyed to anxious.

We rounded a corner as the red-tinged security lights came on and nearly collided with another cluster of delegates, their security detail forming a protective knot around them as they scurried past.

Our designated secure room was three doors down, marked with a discreet placard and guarded by two more members of my detail who stepped aside the moment they saw us coming. Henry pushed through the door and released my arm.

The room was windowless, and the emergency light bathed the space in a harsh neon yellow glow. Decorated with all the warmth of a dentist's waiting room, the only item of interest was the host of surveillance equipment against the far wall.

"Sit," Henry commanded, moving to the bank of monitors showing various security camera feeds.

"Ruff, ruff," I mocked him scornfully, but sat in one of the plain gray metal chairs. On the screens, there were live feeds of the front entrance of the conference center, the street outside, and—

"Is that smoke?" I pointed to one of the monitors.

"Yeah." Henry tapped his earpiece, listening. His expression shifted from alert to relieved. "Copy that. Keep me updated."

He glanced back at me, and the professional mask slipped just slightly. "Initial assessment is that this is a simple car accident. Someone ran off the road and hit a light pole about half a block from the building."

"So nothing to do with the climate conference or the protests?" Relief washed through me, sweet and slightly embarrassing. "We can continue the session?"

"Oh, you weren't done?" Henry asked tartly, his gaze back on the monitors. "Because it really seemed like you were done."

"Madame First Lady!" The Canadian delegate ducked into the room, waving like a friendly scarecrow. "Helena, I'm so glad I caught you!"

I turned, managing not to grimace at the title. Jacob Blackstone was one of the few people at this event who was actually tolerable as a human being. He was also taller than I was, which I appreciated.

Jacob brushed his thinning hair from his forehead with an exaggerated grimace as he folded his narrow frame into the chair beside me. "Darla would have bitten my head off if I missed you."

A quiet laugh escaped me. "That seems unlikely." His wife was literally a foot shorter than he was and so nice it made my teeth ache.

Jacob smiled mischievously. "I have been firmly tasked with getting you to agree to join us for dinner this evening and I shudder to think of facing her wrath if I fail in my mission," he stated dramatically, his mellow baritone drawing out those long Canadian syllables.

"That sounds lovely," I said, and I almost meant it. I was exhausted and just wanted to crash in my room this evening, but Jacob and his wife were the kind of people who made these endless summits bearable. "Can you have a member of your staff send the details to Henry?"

A barrel of a man appeared at Jacob's shoulder. "We should move, sir," he said with a quiet intensity.

Jacob and I both jumped. How did these security folks do this? I cut my gaze at Henry in time to catch the little quirk at the corner of his mouth. I harrumphed and, although his face didn't move, I knew he was laughing at me.

"Dan!" Jacob recovered first. "Perfect timing, as always. Can you coordinate with Henry here about Helena joining us for dinner this evening?"

Dan and Henry exchanged professional nods. Turning back to Jacob, Dan kept his voice low but firm. "The car from earlier has been cleared but the protests outside of the building are escalating. The chair has decided to call it a day. We need to go now, sir."

Jacob threw up his hands in exasperation. "This is Paris, my good man. Protesting is their national pastime."

"I must insist, sir," Dan swept his arm toward the door and Jacob turned back toward me with a sigh.

"I'm so sorry, Helena." He rose and shot a look of censure toward his Chief of Security, who grasped him firmly by the elbow and began steering the much taller man toward the door. "I'll see you this evening!" Jacob called over his shoulder as Dan frog marched him away.

I glanced over at Henry to commiserate, but he was scanning the monitors with one hand over his earpiece. When he finally met my gaze, there was a tiny vertical line pinched between his dark brows.

"Dan wasn't kidding," he said, wrapping a hand around my arm just above my elbow. "We're heading out, too."

He hustled me after the other men and we joined the flow of delegates heading through the big double doors, two agents ahead and two behind.

Outside, the usual Parisian affair of organized chanting and clever signs we'd passed on our way into the building that morning had been replaced by a screaming mob. Clouds of white mist floated across the circle in front of the building, carrying the scents of tear gas and BO.

On either side of the exit, rows of French police officers held the line. Bodies pressed against the other side of their barricades, a seething mass of humanity radiating anger.

"This seems excessive," I choked out, ducking my head as my security detail closed ranks around me. Up ahead the limousine waited at the curb, its door already open.

Then I was in the car, leather seat cool against my legs, and Henry was sliding in beside me. The door slammed shut, muffling the chaos to a dull roar.

The car lurched forward and Henry turned to me with a frown. "They seem angrier than usual."

"No shit," I agreed. "That was a bit much, even for the French. Were there any red flags on today's security briefing?"

"It hasn't come in yet." We were six hours ahead of DC, so it was well into the afternoon here before we got the daily update.

Usually that wasn't an issue.

I pulled out my phone and scanned through the major network headlines, looking for any mentions of Paris, climate activists, general protests, and saw nothing. The updated flu numbers weren't comforting, but there were no new terrorist threats.

I tucked the phone back into my bag and Henry caught my gaze.

"That was quite a performance earlier," he noted.

"Thanks," I responded, leaning my head back and closing my eyes.

"That wasn't really a compliment." Henry's voice was tight and I could imagine the side-eye he was sending my way. "You know they were streaming this thing, right? You just called the President of the United States an idiot on a live feed."

Now my eyes popped open, my gaze meeting his. "I said his *policies* were idiotic. There's a subtle but important distinction."

His mouth twitched. "Oh, I'm sure that will make all the difference to the President."

I leaned my head back, studying the subtly textured fabric of the car's headliner. "What is he going to do, fire me?"

2

Friday Evening

I slipped my favorite earrings in and stepped back to check my outfit. The wide gold hoops were plain but elegant, a gift from my husband on my fifty-ninth birthday. We'd gone out to dinner and he'd talked about throwing a big party for my sixtieth.

I ran a hand over the warm metal. They were his last gift. I was a widow by the time my sixtieth rolled around. There had been no party.

There was a pretty little writing desk in the corner of the suite with a cream leather top. I dropped down into the matching bow-legged chair and picked up the English newspaper I'd been reading earlier and shook my head.

The lead article quoted the head of the CDC, who thought that prion diseases were the same as airborne viruses.

"What a loon," I muttered.

There was a perfunctory knock at the door and my assistant Grace appeared. Her lips were pressed together and her face was pale, mascara smudged at the corners of her eyes. She held out a secure tablet and I took it from her trembling hand.

"What fresh hell is this?" I asked with a frown.

"You have a call from the President," she replied, her eyes communicating volumes, as she slipped back out the door.

"This should be fun," I drawled to the empty room.

I used my thumbprint to access the secure tablet, which immediately displayed an official seal and a spinning icon.

A moment later, the screen switched to an interior shot of the Oval Office.

The President was a rather round man, which made him seem shorter than he actually was, sitting behind the Resolute Desk. When he'd been my husband's VP, I'd spent many a formal function standing beside the man. If only I'd known then what a snake hid behind that porcine facade.

"Good morning, Helena," he began with a frown. His eyes were red as if he hadn't slept.

"It's afternoon here, Calvin," I pointed out with a wide smile. "Have you called to discuss how inept your CDC Director is?"

His frown deepened as he looked down at the notes on the table before him. He picked up the paper with one hand and tugged at his collar with the other.

"The world is safer and our future more secure because of the tireless effort and grace with which you have represented the United States of America." His voice was oddly flat as he read from the document. He paused and his eyes tracked lower before he began again. "After deep reflection and consultation with my advisors, it is my duty to inform you that your mandate as a Special Presidential Envoy is now fulfilled."

Calvin's eyes moved over paragraphs of text and settled toward the bottom of the page. "Your formal duties as an envoy will be officially concluded upon your return from your current assignment. Thank you for your service."

The transmission ended abruptly and I sat in shocked silence for a full minute.

"Thank you for your service?" I repeated incredulously. "You bastard."

There was another brief knock at the door and Grace pushed back into the room, her face strained. "Helena." Her voice cracked. "Everyone's leaving. What are we going to do?"

I sighed, setting the tablet down on the desk. "For Christ's sake, Grace. Take a chill pill. It's not the end of the world."

"The entire security team is on their way to the airport," she flung out one hand dramatically. "Everyone has to be on the next flight to Washington or their positions will be terminated. Henry and I are the only ones allowed to stay and fly back with you tomorrow."

I tapped my chin, my mind still processing the implications.

Henry appeared behind her. His jaw could have cracked walnuts. "They already cut your detail down to the bare minimum before we left DC. This is—"

"Not a surprise," I finished. "This can't be a kneejerk reaction to my faux pas today. It must have been in the works for weeks. The President is simply cleaning house and taking out the trash."

Grace gasped. "Helena!"

"You're a former First Lady," Henry snapped. "You're entitled to Secret Service protection for life. This isn't just disrespectful, it's—"

"Perfectly legal," I interrupted again. I handed the tablet back to Grace with a flip of my wrist, and pulled out my phone, opening up my calendar.

Henry frowned, his eyebrows drawn together like two angry caterpillars about to fight. Or kiss.

Grace took a few steps toward me, clutching at the front of her sweater. "Do you think they'll fire us? What are you doing?"

I clicked a button before looking up at her with a smile. "I'm cancelling my next hair appointment."

"What?" Grace's face collapsed in shock.

"I'm sorry." I pressed my hand to my mouth, but a burst of laughter bubbled up. "I'm sorry, this is just—" I cut myself off. "The President really is an idiot."

"He just fired you," Henry said slowly.

"Exactly!" I spread my arms, feeling something like elation rising in my chest. "I'm free."

They both stared at me.

"After decades of smiling through state dinners and wading through the political crap to try to do some good,

I'm finally free." The words tumbled out faster now. "Two years ago, when John died—"

My voice cracked, and Henry stepped forward. I held up a hand to ward him off.

"When John died," I continued, a tight rein on my emotions. "I couldn't even grieve properly because everyone told me I had to continue to represent his legacy, the office of the President. And now, I am officially absolved of that duty."

"But, Helena," Grace objected. "You've done so much good in this role."

"I'll find other ways to do good, Grace. It's not like I ever really had the personality suited to diplomacy—"

"Agreed," they interrupted me in unison.

I frowned at them both before continuing. "But I'm done with this bullshit. No more power suits, no more blond highlights every six weeks. This is my official retirement." I pulled the pins from my hair, letting the carefully styled waves fall to brush the tops of my shoulders. My scalp tingled with relief. "They may reassign you when we get back, Grace. But first we're going to take a little vacation."

"I can't—"

"You can. You've earned it. We all have." I stood, holding her lightly by the shoulders. "And if they really are stupid enough to fire you when we get back, you'll come work for me. I've had several offers that sounded interesting. Or you could help me write that book we're always talking about. We'll figure it out, okay?"

"Okay." Tears began flowing down Grace's face as she nodded. "Thank you, ma'am," she forced out.

"No, Grace. Thank you." I patted Grace's shoulder as she gave me a wobbly smile. "Let's find a charming inn for a nice long holiday." I opened my laptop and turned to look back over my shoulder at Henry. "And you—?" My voice stuttered to a stop.

He was gone.

3

Friday Night

Perched on a cramped side street off the Champs-Élysées, the restaurant was all polished brass and soft amber lighting that spilled onto the sidewalk like honey. Two members of the Canadian security detail stood flanking the door.

Our car pulled up to the curb and I gathered my clutch. "I'll be fine," I said before Henry could open his mouth.

"Helena—"

"Henry." I turned to face him in the dim interior of the car. "They're Canadians. I couldn't be safer with a busload of nuns."

"The protests—"

"Are over. The conference is done and I'm sure everyone has gone home," I cut him off.

Henry stared at me in silence, his jaw set.

"You are welcome to join us for dinner." I reached for the door handle. "You can sit at the table and enjoy a meal. But you will not stand guard over me for two hours while I eat. Those days are officially over."

His jaw tightened, that little muscle jumping near his ear. "Helena—"

"Stay with the car or join us at the table. Those are your options." I pushed the door open before he could launch into what would undoubtedly be a very thorough explanation of why this was a terrible idea. "I have my phone. I'll text if I need rescuing from excessive politeness."

Sirens wailed in the distance, covering Henry's muttered complaints as I stepped onto the sidewalk, but nothing could dim the tiny burst of happiness in my chest.

I took a deep breath of freedom.

Unfortunately, freedom had the bouquet of a very old city, which was mostly trash and sewage.

Inside the restaurant was surprisingly empty, but the aromas were an immense improvement. As I walked between the quiet tables, I was wrapped in scents of butter and wine and herbs that made my stomach growl despite my exhaustion. Crystal chandeliers cast prisms of light across white tablecloths, and soft conversation hummed beneath the gentle clink of silverware.

"Helena!" Jacob lurched to his feet, nearly knocking over a pitcher of water. "You made it!"

"Of course." I accepted his enthusiastic handshake, which turned into an equally enthusiastic one-armed hug.

Darla rose more gracefully, moving around the table to steal me from her husband, her glossy blonde bob swinging merrily. "Helena, you look so tall and pretty! I love that dress!" She grasped both of my hands in hers and smiled up at me, her face open and friendly. "I'm so happy you could make it. I couldn't stand the thought of not getting to see you this trip." She leaned in to whisper, "I threatened violence," as if scandalized by her own temerity.

"So I heard," I whispered back, charmed despite myself. I let her pull me to a seat. As I slid my chair under the table, my foot hit something soft.

"Ow! You kicked me," came the cry from under the table. "Help! I've been kicked!"

"William." Jacob's voice was a drawn out sigh of parental disappointment. "Is that where you're supposed to be?"

I pulled back the tablecloth, taking in the small boy crouched beneath. "Hello, William. How nice to see you again," I lied.

"Get your big, pointy feet out of my fort," he demanded.

"We talked about this, son," Jacob said mildly, reaching down to retrieve three napkins, a dinner roll, and inexplicably, a red cowboy boot from under the table before extracting a small boy with a mop of golden brown curls and an impressive frown.

William stood next to the table and pulled down the jacket of his little suit, utterly adorable in that sticky way of human children. Then he climbed back into his chair in the most awkward fashion possible. He put one foot on the seat, then the other, and executed a turn while folding one knee under him. William then used both hands to pry his other leg out from under himself until his bottom finally plopped down into the chair with an audible thump that had several of the nearby diners turning their heads.

"We have to be prepared. The French might attack at any moment!" William's surprisingly gruff little voice carried across half the restaurant, and an elderly couple several tables over exchanged alarmed glances.

"I don't think anyone is planning an invasion at this particular time," I said, settling back into my chair.

William turned his attention to me, his dark eyes going wide. "Do I know you? Are you the President of the United States?"

"No, I am not. My name is Helena."

"*Were* you the President?"

"Still no."

He considered this, his nose wrinkling. "Mr. Dan called you the First Person of the United States. Isn't that the President?"

I nodded, understanding. "I was the First *Lady*, because I was married to the President."

"But you aren't anymore?" He squinted at me.

"No, not anymore," I confirmed gently. "That was a long time ago. I'm just a regular person now."

The boy rested his elbows on the table and sighed. "Just another boring grownup."

"Oh, William," Darla said, her cheeks coloring.

"You are absolutely correct." I smiled at William and turned to Darla, patting her hand on the table. "It's okay. I'm quite happy to be boring these days."

Having lost interest in me, William scrambled back under the table, causing it to rock alarmingly and nearly upending the water pitcher. Darla caught it with the reflexes of a seasoned parent and raised a hand to catch someone's attention behind me.

"Sorry about the chaos, Helena," Jacob said, his brow furrowing. "We seem to be going through a bit of a phase lately." Dan appeared beside us and Jacob waved toward the table, which continued to shift alarmingly. "I think William has quite had it for the day, Dan. If you could be so good as to take him back to his nanny, he can have dinner in the room."

With military precision, Dan swept aside the tablecloth and extracted the boy out from underneath. Clutched like a sack of potatoes under Dan's arm, William disappeared before he could get out a protest and the waiter cleared his mess with practiced ease. In short order the three of us were perusing the menu and sipping mineral water in blessed silence.

"We're trying to encourage independence and creativity," Darla explained, smoothing her napkin across her lap. She frowned at me earnestly. "Although honestly at the moment we seem to just be encouraging property damage."

The waiter returned with a Bordeaux that probably cost more than my first car and we ordered.

"So," Jacob said, once our glasses were filled. "I heard some news this evening."

I swirled the wine in my glass. There were reds and pale golds running through the liquid and every now and then, a glimpse of the deepest purple. "Did you?" I prompted before lifting the glass to my lips.

"The grapevine says you're stepping back from your official role."

The wine was rich and smooth against my tongue, with notes of blackberry. "Wow. Good news travels fast."

Jacob's usual jovial expression had softened into something more serious, though his eyes still crinkled at the corners. "For what it's worth, Helena, I think you've done an amazing job. Truly exceptional work."

Heat crept up my neck. I'd spent thirty years deflecting compliments, redirecting credit, making sure everyone knew it was a team effort. Old habits.

"That's kind of you to say," I forced out.

"It's not kindness, it's fact." He leaned forward slightly, his long fingers wrapping around his wine glass. "There are many of us who know how much work you took on that last year before John died."

The wine turned to ash in my mouth.

"Jacob," Darla murmured, her hand reaching out to touch his arm.

"Thank you," I managed, swallowing down the emotion and forcing a bright smile. "So," I said, my tone much lighter. "Are you two excited to be heading back home tomorrow?"

Darla lit up, her whole face transforming. "Oh, we're having a bit of a family vacation first! We're heading south to Nice for a couple of days of sun and beach and absolutely no politics."

"That sounds lovely," I said warmly, her happiness infectious. "I'm taking a bit of a vacation myself."

"Here in France?" Darla asked.

I nodded, smiling. "At a little bed and breakfast just outside of a tiny village called Saint-Amélie-de-Provence, about an hour from Nice. Family-run, historic building, beautiful gardens, the works." I couldn't hide my excitement, and I didn't try.

Darla sighed, clasping her hands together. "Saint-Amélie-de-Provence," she repeated. "What a charming name. That sounds lovely."

The waiter returned with beautifully plated dishes that belonged in a magazine. I'd ordered the duck, which came with a cherry reduction almost too pretty to eat.

"So what comes next for you after your vacation?" Jacob prodded. "If you don't mind my asking."

I took a bite of duck, savoring the rich meat and the sweet-tart brightness of the cherries.

"Honestly? I have no idea." The admission was terrifying and exhilarating in equal measure. "I've been approached by a publisher about writing a book about my years in the White House and John's administration, but mainly I'm looking forward to being a private citizen again. Sleeping past six. Not having to have an opinion on everything."

"You?" Jacob's eyebrows shot up. "No opinions? I'll believe that when I see it."

I smiled. He wasn't wrong, after all. "Maybe I'll get a dog." I reached for my wine again. The soft clink of dishes, murmured conversations in various languages, and the occasional burst of laughter from the bar all hummed around us.

It was all terribly normal.

We talked for another hour, the conversation drifting from climate policy to favorite books to Darla's passionate defense of a romantic comedy I'd never heard of and which Jacob had found to be complete drivel. The wine kept flowing, and the tight knot of tension that had lived between my shoulder blades for the past two years began to loosen.

"We should let you go," Jacob said finally, glancing at his watch. "It's getting late, and we all have early flights."

"We do." I stood, steadying myself against the table as my exhaustion—and several glasses of wine—finally caught up with me. "This was wonderful. Thank you both so much for the invitation."

Darla stood as well, pulling me into a brief, floral-scented hug. "Take care of yourself, Helena. You've earned it."

"I'll try."

"Don't try," Jacob said, wrapping me in another enthusiastic embrace. "Do. Be selfish. Sleep late. Watch silly movies. Eat ice cream for breakfast."

"That's your retirement plan, is it?" Darla asked him with an affectionate side eye.

"Absolutely."

They were lovely people and I didn't begrudge them their happiness, but it was a relief to finally say goodbye. The night air hit me like a slap when I stepped outside, brisk with the first chill of fall after the warmth of the restaurant. Henry was leaning against the limo already sitting at the curb, somehow managing to look both relaxed and hypervigilant at the same time. His head came up the moment I appeared, and his gaze raked me from head to toe in a quick, professional assessment.

"Good dinner?" he asked, opening the car door.

"I have emerged unscathed." I slid into the backseat. "It was quite pleasant, actually. They really are a nice couple. Their child is a complete menace, though."

"I noticed that," Henry said with just a hint of a snicker as he climbed in behind me and closed the door. He settled onto the opposite bench with his customary economy of movement. The car pulled away from the curb, and the restaurant lights faded behind us.

"I'm going to adopt a dog when I get home," I said to the window.

"How much wine did you have?" Henry asked incredulously.

"Not enough." I turned to look at him, taking in the sharp line of his jaw in the passing streetlights. "I think I'm having a mid-life crisis, Henry."

"You're sixty-two. Isn't it a bit late for mid-life?"

I stared at him balefully. "You bastard."

His mouth quirked. "I try."

4

Saturday Morning

Bright and early the next morning Henry, Grace, and I piled into a taxi and headed for the airport. Brake lights stretched ahead like a string of red Christmas bulbs as we approached Charles de Gaulle. Outside my window, sirens wailed as morning commuters hunched against the wind, their coats pulled tight.

"This traffic is ridiculous," Grace muttered, leaning forward between the front seats to peer through the windshield. She sat back, arms folded across her chest. "I can't believe we have to take a public cab back to the airport."

Henry shrugged from where he sat in the front passenger seat. "The traffic would have been just as bad in the limo."

The driver inched us forward until the lights changed again. A motorcycle zipped past, close enough that I could have touched it, the engine whine cutting through the sealed windows. The rider wove between cars with a complete lack of self-preservation.

"At least we left early," I said, turning away from the window with a sigh. "Even after all of those closed roads and detours, we still have plenty of time before the flight."

"The city makes everyone crazy," Grace sighed.

I nodded. "I won't miss it."

We'd reached the departures ramp, the road curving up toward the terminal. Traffic had slowed in the oncoming lanes and was moving carefully around two cars pulled off onto the far side of the road.

Our light changed and the taxi pulled closer. As we inched past the scene, two men grappled on the pavement, a tangle of limbs and flying fists. The bigger of the two men had the other in a choke hold, his arm locked around the other man's throat. The trapped man's face had gone purple, his hands clawing at the arm cutting off his air.

"Looks like they need a vacation, too," I muttered.

"I don't think a vacation is going to fix that," Henry said, as the taxi pulled past them and into the terminal dropoff zone.

***

Ashley

The plane touched down and Ashley's stomach followed a long moment later. She grabbed Robert's arm, his bicep warm and solid under her fingers. Her heart fluttered in her chest at the contact.

"Easy there, Ash," Robert said, patting her hand without looking up from his phone. "Just turbulence."

"I know, I know." She released him reluctantly, smoothing down the front of the cream-colored cashmere sweater he'd bought her for her twenty-fifth birthday last month. "I'm just excited to finally be here! Paris!"

She pressed her nose against the cold glass. Only tarmac surrounded them, gray and endless. But it was French tarmac and that was enough to make it fascinating.

Robert unbuckled his seatbelt, reaching for his carry-on in the overhead bin. His movements were sharp, efficient, the same way he moved through the office.

"The seatbelt light is still on," she whispered, glancing around at the other passengers who were all still seated. "We're supposed to wait."

"I want to get through customs before the unwashed masses." He pulled down his leather bag with a grunt.

The plane lurched to a stop and the seatbelt light turned off with a ding. Suddenly everyone was standing, the aisle clogged with bodies. Robert pushed forward, using his shoulders to create space, and Ashley scrambled after him, clutching her other birthday gift, a large leather purse, to her chest.

"Excuse me, sorry, pardon me," she murmured as she squeezed past a woman with approximately seventeen shopping bags and a man who reeked of cologne and pretzels.

The jet bridge was shockingly warm, the recycled air mixed with industrial cleaner fumes. Ashley's Louboutins clicked along the hard surface of the hallway, pinching her feet. After twelve hours of travel her toes were small, angry sausages stuffed into their designer casings.

"Keep up, Ashley," Robert called over his shoulder, not slowing down.

"I'm trying!" The words came out breathy and she quickened her pace, ankles wobbling dangerously. These shoes were not meant for speed-walking through international airports, she thought regretfully.

Charles de Gaulle unfolded before them in a maze of sleek modernity. People rushed past in both directions, wheeling suitcases and shouting into phones in a dozen different languages. A baby let out a skull-piercing cry somewhere to the left.

"Robert, wait—" But he was already ten feet ahead, his gray suit jacket barely wrinkled despite the flight. Ashley looked down at her own outfit, creased and lived in.

She caught up to Robert at the customs queue, which snaked back and forth like an angry serpent. The line seemed to be at a standstill and Robert's jaw was tight.

"This is ridiculous," he muttered, checking his Rolex. "We've been standing here for ten minutes."

It had been less than two, but she didn't correct him. "At least we're here together," she offered, looping her arm through his. "Our romantic getaway!"

He glanced at her, the corners of his mouth turning down. "Right."

The couple in front of them was arguing in rapid-fire French, their hands gesturing wildly. Behind, someone's phone kept chiming with notifications, the same cheerful ding over and over.

"I'm so sad the girls couldn't come," Ashley said, trying again. "I'm dying to meet them."

Robert's expression hardened, his shoulders going rigid. "Yeah, well, there's no way my bitch of an ex-wife would have allowed that."

"Robert—"

"We're supposed to have shared custody, but I still have to pay child support. How does that make sense?" His voice rose as he started down this familiar rant and the couple in front of them stopped arguing to glance back.

"That's awful," she agreed quickly, squeezing his arm. "I'm so sorry she's being unreasonable."

"You have no idea." He ran a hand through his carefully moussed dark hair. "Twenty years I gave that woman. And this is how she repays me. Taking my money—"

"Next!" The customs agent was waving them forward, his expression shifting from bored to annoyed.

Robert stepped up to the counter, both passports in hand. With his shoulders back and chin up, he was every inch the successful CEO. The agent barely glanced at the passports before stamping them and waving them through. Robert just had that effect on people.

Baggage claim was chaos. The area was packed with people, most of whom were crowded around the carousels and the rest standing in front of the large television screens, staring at the news. The big luggage conveyors groaned and creaked as they slowly rotated, spitting out suitcases at random intervals. A small child bounced off Ashley's legs and careened away.

Robert spotted his sleek black suitcase and hauled it off the belt with a grunt. Impatience radiated from him as they waited for Ashley's pink hard-shell to finally appear. When it did, she lunged for it, but couldn't maneuver the bulky shape off the belt before it was swept away. Robert's annoyance was a physical presence as she waited for the bag to come around again.

"Got it!" She wrestled it onto the floor, her shoulder screaming in protest. Robert was already walking toward the exit.

"Robert!" But he was too far ahead to hear. She struggled to extend the handle, sighing in relief as it finally clicked into place. She rolled it in the direction Robert had disappeared, the wheels clicking over the tile in a rhythm that matched the throbbing of her feet.

She found him standing under a bank of blue signage announcing connecting flights and the various exit points of the airport. To the right a screen showed a frowning news anchor, but the French captions scrolled by too quickly for Ashley to catch.

"I can't wait to practice my French," she told Robert, her excitement building again. "I'm so rusty."

He didn't look down at her. "Is a driver picking us up or did you rent a car?"

"I rented a car." She pointed toward the sign bearing the logos of the various rental companies. "That way."

The next sign over, displaying the connecting flight gates, flickered. The first flight shifted to red, then the next, and the next. The change cascaded down the board until every flight was listed as canceled.

"Huh," she said. "That's weird."

"What?" Robert was looking at his phone.

"Look." She waved her arm toward the board. "All the flights are canceled."

"Probably another strike." He wrapped a hand around her arm. "Let's get out of here."

A woman brushed past them, moving fast, her face pale and drawn. She was crying, mascara running down her cheeks in dark rivulets. Behind her, a family argued loudly in German or maybe Dutch, their voices sharp and angry. Robert maneuvered them through the crowds and within minutes they were heading toward the garage, rental car keys in hand.

"I hope this doesn't become another lockdown." Ashley scanned the crowded concourse, noting how many people were sporting masks.

The automatic doors whooshed open and they stepped out into the cool morning air. The sky was gray, but Ashley's tired body was suddenly full of excitement.

"Oh my god," she gushed. "We're actually in Paris."

"So," Robert said as they walked the line of rental cars. "Where exactly is this hotel?"

"It's not a hotel!" Ashley bounced on her sore toes, unable to contain her excitement despite his tone. "It's a bed and breakfast. A real authentic French inn! I found it on this amazing blog about hidden gems in Provence. It's so charming—stone walls, gardens, home-cooked meals—"

"Provence." Robert's voice was flat. "Isn't that at the other end of the country?"

"It's about nine hours south!" She beamed at him. "Everyone does Paris. I thought we could do something different. Something special."

His jaw tightened again. "Nine hours."

"We'll split the drive up over a couple of days, so we can see the countryside. I rented a convertible!" She pulled up the rental confirmation on her phone, showing him the picture of a sleek red Audi. "Top of the line. We can stop at little cafes, visit some lavender fields—"

"Lavender fields." He said it like she'd suggested they tour a sewage treatment plant.

"Robert, come on. Don't be like that." Ashley slipped her arm through his again, pressing close. "It'll be romantic. Just the two of us, the open road, the wind in our hair, beautiful scenery—"

He looked down at her, his expression a blank mask for a beat too long. Just as a bead of sweat began to form at the small of Ashley's back, his expression lightened.

"You're right," he said, his lips turning up at the corners. "It'll be an adventure."

"Really?" Relief flooded through her, warm and sweet. "You're not mad?"

"Why would I be mad?" The smile didn't quite reach his eyes. "You went to all this trouble to plan something special."

The rental car facility was in a massive concrete structure that echoed with engine noise and shouted conversations. They took an elevator down three levels, the fluorescent lights humming overhead and making everything slightly green and sickly. Ashley's reflection in the metal doors showed dark circles under her eyes that her concealer was no longer concealing.

"This way," she said, leading Robert through a maze of identical-looking aisles. Their footsteps echoed off the low ceiling.

The Audi was perfect. Cherry red, sleek and low to the ground, the soft top already folded down. Ashley ran a hand along the hood, warm under her palm even in the cool garage air.

"What do you think?" she asked, turning to Robert with a grin.

"It'll do." But he was circling it, checking the tires, peering in the windows, warming to it despite himself.

Men and their cars, Ashley thought indulgently.

"It's perfect," she insisted, popping the trunk to load the bags.

The space was tiny and she had to rearrange the suitcases three times before it would close. Robert stood by the side of the car, frowning at his phone.

With a sigh she slammed the trunk shut and offered Robert the keys. "Ready?"

He moved to the passenger side. "You drive. I need to get some work done."

Ashley didn't try to hide her sigh of contentment as she slid into the buttery leather of the driver's seat.

"This is going to be so much fun," she said brightly, starting the engine. It purred to life, smooth and powerful.

Robert didn't look up from his phone. "Let's go."

The GPS took a moment to load, the screen flickering before settling down. Just over four hours to the cute little boutique hotel where they'd be spending the night. The route glowed blue on the screen, winding south through what the map promised would be beautiful countryside.

Ashley pulled the car carefully out of the tight space, her hands gripping the wheel hard enough to make her knuckles white. The Audi was only slightly bigger than her Honda Civic back home, but she'd never driven a car this expensive. She tapped the brake a little too hard and it jerked to a stop.

"Easy there, Speed Racer," Robert muttered.

"I've got it." She crept forward at approximately one mile per hour, positive she was going to scrape the pristine paint job on one of the concrete pillars that seemed to be multiplying around them.

Finally, blessedly, the car was free and heading toward the exit ramp. She followed the signs for the highway, her eyes darting between the GPS, the road, and the plethora of traffic signs in multiple languages.

Her foot came off the gas as they approached a row of emergency vehicles parked beside the ramp, lights flashing. There were police cars and two ambulances.

"I hope everyone is okay," Ashley said with a frown, downshifting to slow the car to a crawl.

"Not our problem. Drive, Ashley."

At the back of the second ambulance, several people, including a couple of uniformed officers, were rolling across the oil-stained concrete. One of them was screaming something in French, the words ragged and desperate. A woman stood nearby, frozen, her hands pressed to her mouth.

Ashley pressed on the gas, guiding the car past the scene.

"Jesus," Robert scoffed. "The French are so dramatic."

46

5

Saturday Afternoon

Helena

When the plane touched down, I pulled my phone out of my pocket to turn it back on. I sat in my seat, staring at the black screen for a long moment. Who would be calling me?

I slipped the phone back into my carryon and exited the plane, the screen still dark.

We met the car Grace had arranged and set off down the highway. Henry and Grace pulled out their phones, expressions intent, but I cracked my window and watched the world go by. As we crossed over a bridge I caught a glimpse of the Mediterranean in the distance.

After about an hour we left the highway, and drove through a picturesque little medieval village full of narrow streets and stone buildings. Grace looked up from her phone to gasp in appreciation as we passed under a stone arch. A mile or two past the town, we rounded a gentle curve and the inn materialized like something from a postcard. Three stories of honey-colored stone, blue shutters that echoed the hues of the distant mountains, and a real terracotta tile roof that sagged gently in the middle with age.

It had been gray and rainy in Paris. Here the sky was blue and the ivy climbing the exterior was green and lush. Window boxes still overflowed with the flowers of summer—geraniums in shades of pink and red, their petals looking slightly worn but relentlessly cheerful.

"Oh, this is perfect," Grace said. "It's like something out of a movie." She was already unbuckling her seatbelt as the cab passed between two tall stone pillars and entered a small gravel courtyard where a few cars were neatly parked in a row along to the right.

As the car rolled to a stop, a small herd of at least a dozen or so tiny goats appeared from behind the house. They were mostly white with brown patches, and moved toward us with purpose.

The driver tapped his horn and the lead goat, no taller than knee height, froze, all four legs jutting out straight from his body. His momentum carried him forward and he tumbled head over hooves.

We all sat there for a moment, frozen, as each tiny goat rocked and rolled across the grass. Some of the goats swung right back up onto their hooves, but others took a few seconds. The lead goat didn't even shake off his fall. He just rocked back up onto his feet and made a beeline toward the other side of the large house, his friends following in his wake. A tiny white goat was the last one to recover and he rushed to catch up, bleating desperately as he followed the herd's path and disappeared from sight.

Our driver muttered something that sounded like *"putain de chèvres"* as he swung open his door. He rounded the car to pop the trunk and began unloading our luggage onto the gravel.

"Huh," Henry grunted. He shook his head and exited the car, scanning the property intently.

I climbed out more slowly, my joints protesting after yet another day of sitting, first the flight and then the car ride. But the sky was blue and the air carried scents of rosemary and thyme. Grabbing my bag, I turned toward the house as the car drove away.

A large white cat was sprawled artfully across the stone steps leading to the front door, his bright yellow eyes tracking our approach.

"Hello, there," I said cautiously.

The cat's eyes blinked slowly in his rather flat face, and he stood, stretched in that boneless way cats have, and undulated across the tile, rolls of white fur shifting with each step. As he got closer I glanced from his fluffy white body to my navy slacks with a frown and took a large step back.

"I'm not really a cat person—"

The cat's ears flattened against his skull. His mouth opened to reveal tiny sharp teeth as he hissed.

Henry appeared beside me, suitcases in both hands. "Already offending the locals?"

"That's a big cat," Grace said diplomatically, giving him a wide berth.

The cat's attention shifted to Grace. His ears perked forward, his expression transforming from murderous to adoring in the space of a heartbeat. He trotted toward her with surprising speed for something that resembled a furry ottoman and began weaving between her legs, purring loudly enough to rattle windows.

"Oh!" Grace set down her bag and crouched, running her hand along the cat's broad back. "Aren't you handsome!"

"Be careful," I cautioned, and was ignored.

"He's so precious," Grace cooed, scratching behind his ears. The cat's purr increased in volume, a sound like a diesel engine idling.

"He's discriminating," Henry said, his mouth twitching.

Before I could formulate a properly scathing response, the front door burst open with enough force to send it crashing against the exterior wall.

"*Bienvenue!* Welcome!"

The woman who emerged was a force of nature compressed into about five feet four inches of pure theatrical energy. She was probably around my age, but her hair was an improbable shade of red, styled in soft whispy waves that framed a face dominated by bold red-painted lips. She wore a flowing caftan in shades of purple and gold that caught the breeze like a sail, and enough jewelry to stock a small boutique—gold bangles on both wrists, multiple chains around her neck, and earrings that nearly brushed her shoulders.

"You must be the Americans!" She descended the steps with her arms spread wide, bracelets jangling. "The Barretts! How wonderful, how absolutely marvelous that you have come to us!"

She swept toward Henry, grasping both his hands in hers. "Ah, this must be Monsieur Barrett. What a handsome man you are! So distinguished," She paused, her head tilting as she studied his face. "So serious. We will fix this, yes? A few days at *La Maison des Fleurs* and you will smile again."

Henry's expression suggested he'd rather face down an armed insurgent than this enthusiastic whirlwind of a woman. "Ma'am, I'm not—"

"Please, please, you must call me Begonia!" She released his hands only to pat his cheek. "We are all friends here, yes? No formality, no stuffiness. You are on holiday!"

"We're not married," I interjected, moving closer. The cat, still wrapped around Grace's legs, hissed at me again. "I'm Helena Barrett." I waved a hand toward Henry's put-upon expression. "This is Henry."

Begonia's hands flew to her mouth, her eyes going wide. "Oh! I see—" She turned to me, her expression transforming from mortified to speculative in the span of a heartbeat. "So this is a secret weekend, yes? A little naughty?"

"No," Henry and I said in unison.

Begonia laughed, a rich, melodious sound that seemed to roll across the courtyard. "Of course, of course. Forgive me, I am a hopeless romantic. I recall now that you have booked three separate rooms." She looked quite sad about that for just a moment before brightening again. "But you, Monsieur Henry, you are single, yes?"

"I'm here to work," Henry said flatly.

"Work? Work!" Begonia waved a dismissive hand, her bangles chiming. "This is France, *mon cher*. We live, we love, we enjoy the good things in life."

She moved closer to him and I snapped.

"He's not interested," I said, my voice sharper than I'd intended. Three pairs of eyes swiveled toward me. Even the cat stopped purring and turned to stare.

Begonia's perfectly arched eyebrows rose. "Ah," she said, drawing out the syllable. "I see."

"I doubt it," I said with a frown.

Henry shifted the grip she held on his hand to shake it firmly, once, before letting go. "Henry O'Connell, ma'am. I'm Mrs. Barrett's head of security." He turned toward Grace. "And this is Grace Diaz, Mrs. Barrett's assistant."

"Ohh, how intriguing," Begonia cooed, but her smile suggested she didn't believe a word of it. She clapped her hands together, the sound sharp in the quiet courtyard. "Well then! Let me show you to your rooms, yes? You must be exhausted from your journey."

She turned toward the house, her caftan billowing behind her like a ship's sail and Henry shot me a look that promised retribution as he grabbed the suitcases. Grace scooped up her own bag, the cat protesting loudly as she moved away from him. The animal fixed me with another baleful glare before stalking off toward the side of the house where the goats had disappeared, his tail held high in indignation.

"Oh, yeah. I definitely feel relaxed," I muttered.

The interior of La Maison des Fleurs was everything the exterior had promised. Exposed beams ran across the high ceiling above terracotta floors. The walls were whitewashed plaster, and the furniture managed to be both rustic and elegant. The air was infused with lavender and baked goods, warm and yeasty and welcoming.

"The house has been in my late husband's family for two hundred years," Begonia explained as she led us into the lobby, dominated by an enormous stone fireplace. "We have modernized, of course—the bathrooms, the kitchen, the wifi—but we have kept the soul of the place, yes? The history."

"It's beautiful," Grace said, craning her neck to take everything in.

"*Merci, chérie.*" Begonia paused at the base of a wide staircase, one hand on the carved newel post. "Now, I have given you our best rooms. For Madame Barrett, our best suite, with its own private balcony and a lovely view."

She started up the stairs, still talking. "Breakfast is served from eight to ten, but if you sleep late, no matter! I will make you something. Lunch you are on your own—there are wonderful restaurants and cafes in the village, or I can prepare a basket for a picnic. Dinner is at eight on the terrace."

We reached the second floor landing and Begonia gestured down a hallway lined with doors. "Grace, you are here. Henry, you are in the next room." She opened both doors and then crossed to the other side of the hallway, and pushed into the final room with a flourish.

"*Voilà!* Your sanctuary, Madame Barrett."

The room was perfect. A large four-poster bed dominated the space, dressed in white linens that looked crisp and inviting. French doors opened onto a small balcony, and through them I could see fields stretching toward distant hills. The walls were a lovely soft yellow, and exposed beams crossed the ceiling. A pretty little table stood beneath one window, and a comfortable-looking chair with an ottoman occupied the corner near the fireplace.

"The bathroom is through there," Begonia said, pointing to a door on the left. "I have put out fresh towels, and there is a robe in the closet. If you need anything, anything at all, you simply pick up the phone—" She indicated an old-fashioned rotary phone on the bedside table. "—and dial zero. I will answer, day or night."

"Thank you," I said, setting my purse on the desk. "This is lovely."

"It is my favorite room," Begonia confided, moving to the French doors and pushing them open. Fresh air flooded in, carrying the scent of lavender and warm earth.

I joined her on the small balcony, taking in the view of the garden below us. In the distance the lavender fields were beginning to fade from their summer purple to a dustier shade, but they were still beautiful, rolling away toward the mountains in neat rows.

"It's peaceful," I said quietly.

"Yes." Begonia was silent for a moment, her effervescence dimmed as she gazed down into the garden. "My husband proposed to me beneath that tree. Nearly forty years ago, can you imagine?"

"It's a beautiful spot," I said.

"It is, yes?" She smiled, but there was sadness in it. "He's been gone for nearly twenty years."

"I'm sorry."

She waved a hand, her bangles jangling. "It is life, no? We love, we lose, we continue." Her gaze dropped to my left hand, where my wedding ring caught the afternoon light. "You understand this, I think."

I looked down at the ring, the simple gold band that circled my finger. "My husband died two years ago."

"Ah." Begonia reached out and took my hand, holding it gently in both of hers. "And you still wear the ring."

"I do." I didn't try to explain it, didn't try to justify it. It was simply true.

Begonia hesitated, before smiling sheepishly. "I recognize you now. Your husband was the American President, was he not?"

I sighed. So much for anonymity. "Yes."

"*Mon Dieu.*" Begonia's hands tightened on mine. "You are here, in my little inn. How exciting!" She pressed her lips together, making a visible effort to gather her composure. "I am sorry. I am being foolish. You came here for privacy, for peace, and here I am making a fuss."

"It's all right," I said, and was surprised to find I meant it. There was something genuine in her reaction, something that felt more like recognition than pandering.

"I admired your husband very much," Begonia said quietly. "He seemed to be a man of honor, of compassion."

My throat tightened. "He was," I managed.

We stood there for a moment, two widows on a balcony in Provence.

"Does it get better?" I asked, the question escaping before I could stop it. "Everyone keeps telling me it will, but—"

"Do you want me to lie?" Begonia asked with a small smile.

I let out a breath that was almost a laugh. "Yes. Lie to me, please."

"Come now," Begonia chided me gently, patting my hand once before releasing it and moving toward the door. "You are made of stronger stuff than that."

"I'm tired," I admitted.

"Then rest," she said simply. "That is why you are here."

6

Saturday Evening

For a disorienting moment, I had no idea where I was. Then the lavender-scented pillows registered, followed by the distant bleating of those ridiculous goats.

Vacation.

I fumbled for my phone on the nightstand, but it was still sitting dead in my bag. There was an old fashioned alarm clock, the glowing red numbers announcing that it was dinner time. I'd laid on the bed to close my eyes for just a moment and apparently fallen asleep for nearly four hours.

Vacation, damn it.

"Shit," I muttered, flopping onto my back and slapping a hand over my forehead. After just one more minute of wallowing, I sat up and ran my hands through my hair. I'd fallen asleep in my sweater set and slacks, which were now hopelessly creased.

I could just stay here. Order room service. Except this wasn't a chain hotel, and I was fairly certain my flamboyant hostess would take it as a personal insult if I didn't join everyone for dinner. Worse, she'd probably come up here and drag me down herself, caftan waving behind her like the French version of a superhero's cape.

A sharp knock at the door interrupted my internal debate.

"Helena." Henry's voice carried through the wood. "Don't even think about not coming down to dinner."

"Go away," I called back hoarsely. "I'm on vacation."

"You're not hiding in your room all night."

I marched over to the door and swung it open. "I'm not hiding," I protested, outraged. "I took a nap."

Henry's eyebrows shot up and he looked at me dubiously. "Well, you're up now. You might as well come down and eat something."

"You're not my mother," I muttered like a mature adult.

"Thank God for that. Change your clothes and come downstairs."

I opened my mouth to tell him exactly where he could shove his suggestions, but he turned on his heel and took himself off down the hall. Bastard.

My suitcase sat on the luggage rack, still partially packed. I pulled out a pair of dark wool trousers, a simple white linen blouse, and a cabled navy cardigan. The mirror over the dresser showed a woman who looked a little pale but presentable. I twisted my hair up into a loose knot, securing it with a clip, and added a swipe of lipstick.

"Good enough," I told my reflection.

The stairs creaked under my feet as I descended, the sound oddly comforting. A low hum of chatter grew as I crossed the lobby to where light spilled through open French doors onto a tiled terrace.

The scene that greeted me was something straight out of a magazine spread. Fairy lights were strung overhead in swooping arcs, casting everything in a warm, golden glow. Large ceramic chimineas stood at intervals around the space, radiating warmth against the cooling evening air. A long wooden table dominated the terrace, already laden with platters and bowls and bottles of wine that caught the light.

Begonia stood at the head of the table in a caftan that made her earlier outfit look positively restrained. This one was emerald green with gold embroidery that caught the light and demanded attention. Her jewelry had multiplied—more bangles, more necklaces, earrings that could double as weapons.

"Ah!" She spotted me and clapped her hands together. "Our honored guest has emerged from her cocoon!"

Every head at the table turned toward me. Wonderful.

"Nope," I said, standing frozen in the doorway. "Just an old lady who overslept."

Begonia laughed, the sound rich and genuine. She crossed to my side and captured one of my hands in hers. "We are of an age, my dear. I am not old, so you cannot be either, I'm afraid." Her eyes traveled over my outfit, one perfectly shaped eyebrow rising. "But we must work on your wardrobe."

I glanced down at myself and shrugged. "We can't all be fashionistas, *madame*."

"How can you breathe?" She gestured at her own flowing dress. "So buttoned up! This is France, *chérie*. We believe in freedom!" She patted my hand. "And you will call me Begonia, and I will call you Helena, yes? And after a few days here, you will be wearing scarves and drinking wine at lunch like a proper French woman."

"I'm not sure my liver can handle that level of commitment."

"But your heart will thank you." Begonia steered me toward the table. "Now, come. Let me introduce you to everyone."

Henry was already seated, a glass of red wine in front of him and an expression that suggested he was reconsidering his life choices. Grace sat beside him, her eyes bright with barely contained excitement. The poor thing probably thought this was all terribly romantic.

"We have your companions, of course," Begonia said. "And here—" She gestured to a young man who'd risen from his seat, his movements awkward but earnest. "—is my son, Jean Luc."

Jean Luc was probably in his mid twenties, tall and lean with strawberry blond waves. He had his mother's good looks but none of her theatrical presence.

"Madame Barrett," he said quietly with a small bow. "It is an honor."

"Please, just Helena." I extended my hand and he shook it gently, like I might break. "It's lovely to meet you."

"Jean Luc helps me run the inn," Begonia explained, her hand resting on her son's shoulder with obvious affection. "He is very good with the business side. Numbers, bookings, all the things that make my head hurt."

"Someone has to keep the lights on," Jean Luc said with a small smile.

"And here—" Begonia moved to the other end of the table where a tiny woman sat, her snow white hair styled in a surprisingly modern pixie cut. "—is Rose, my *belle-mère*. My mother-in-law."

Rose looked up from her wine glass, her eyes sharp and assessing behind wire-rimmed glasses. She was probably in her eighties, barely five feet tall, but something in her expression suggested she could level a man at twenty paces.

"Another American," Rose said in heavily accented English. Her voice was surprisingly strong for someone so small. "You people are everywhere, like cockroaches."

"Rose!" Begonia gasped, a hand flying to her bosom as she sank into her chair.

I barked out a laugh. "It's a fair assessment," I said with a smile, sliding into the empty chair across from her. "We do tend to be an invasive species."

Rose's mouth twitched. "At least you have humor. Most Americans are so serious. Always working, always worried." She took a sip of wine. "It is exhausting just to watch."

"I'm actively trying to be less exhausting."

"This one may have potential." She nodded to Begonia and then swung out a tiny wrinkled hand to gesture at my outfit. "Although she dresses like she's going to a funeral."

"Well, the night is young," I pointed out, raising my eyebrows.

Rose cackled and reached out to slap Begonia's arm. "I like this one. She has spine."

"Of course she has spine. She was married to a president." Begonia filled my wine glass with a generous pour. "Can you imagine? All those stuffy dinners, all those boring politicians. It would kill a lesser woman."

"It nearly killed me," I admitted, accepting the glass. The wine was deep red, almost purple in the fairy lights. I took a sip, savoring the smooth and complex flavor with notes of dark fruit and something earthy I couldn't quite place.

I set the glass down and let my gaze move around the table. The conversation had gone quiet. Even the fairy lights seemed dimmer.

Begonia reached over and covered my hand with hers. Her rings were warm against my skin. "I am so sorry, *chérie.*"

"I'm sorry. I didn't mean to damper the mood." I pulled my hand back gently. "This wine is excellent."

"Of course." Begonia sat back, but her expression was soft with understanding. "It is a local vintage. May I refill your glass?"

"Please, God, yes."

"Well," Grace piped up from down the table, her voice bright with forced cheer. "Where is everyone from?"

I'd barely noticed the other people at the table. An older couple sat near Henry, their expressions polite but reserved. Two young women were seated beside Jean Luc, holding hands under the table in that way new couples do, like they might float away if they let go.

As the older couple introduced themselves and described their home in Munich, Begonia leaned into my space. "They have been coming here for five years, every September," she said softly. "And our young Parisian friends—" She gestured to the young women. "—are on their honeymoon!"

"Congratulations," I said, raising my glass toward them.

They beamed, their faces flushed with wine and happiness.

"Unfortunately, they are all leaving tomorrow," Begonia continued with an exaggerated pout. "So tonight we must celebrate! Tomorrow the *maison* will be very quiet and sad."

"Not too sad," Jean Luc interjected. "We have another couple checking in."

"Ah, yes!" Begonia's face brightened. "More Americans!" She waved her hand vaguely. "From somewhere...your names all sound the same to me."

"That's not offensive at all," I said dryly.

"You know what I mean! New York, California, Texas—it is all hamburgers and baseball, yes?"

"And school shootings and medical bankruptcy," I added.

Rose cackled again, nearly spilling her wine and Begonia turned to me, her expression mock-serious.

"You must loosen up, Helena," she insisted. "Unbutton the top button, at least. Live a little!"

"I'm not unbuttoning anything."

"I blame the Puritans!" She threw up her hands in exasperation, her bangles creating a symphony. "So afraid of a little skin!"

"I'm not afraid. I'm just not interested in giving the paparazzi a reason to photograph me."

"Paparazzi? Here?" Begonia looked around the terrace theatrically. "Where? Behind the geraniums? Hiding in the fig trees?"

"You'd be surprised where they turn up."

"Let them come! I will smack them over the head." She stood, moving to the sideboard where platters of food waited. "Now, enough talking. We eat!"

The food kept coming in waves. There was crusty bread still warm from the oven, creamy cheese that probably violated several health codes, olives that gleamed like jewels, roasted vegetables that smelled like Thanksgiving, and a chicken dish that made my mouth water just looking at it.

"This is incredible," Grace breathed, loading her plate with what appeared to be everything within reach.

"It is simple food," Begonia said with a shrug. "But made with love, yes? This is the secret."

"The secret is butter," Rose interjected.

"Yes, and butter. This is also true," Begonia agreed.

The conversation flowed as easily as the wine. The Germans talked about their grandchildren in careful, precise English while the newlyweds giggled over some private joke. Jean Luc explained the finer points of running an inn to an increasingly interested Grace, who was asking questions like she was thinking of switching careers.

"So," Begonia said, turning her attention back to me. "What is it that you do? Now that you are no longer the First Lady?"

"Well, I was working on climate policy," I explained. "I used to be a teacher and that was important to me."

"Was?" Begonia probed.

"I just wrapped up my last conference," I said shortly.

One of the young women at the end of the table choked back a laugh. When I cut my eyes her way, she smiled widely.

"We saw the video," she said in a lilting accent. "It was wonderful."

Her wife nodded emphatically. "We agree with your sentiment wholeheartedly, Mrs. Barrett."

Henry sighed and shook his head. "Please don't encourage her."

Begonia looked between us all, confused.

"Good," Rose interjected, slanting what could only be described as a leer in Henry's direction. "So now you can focus on husband number two."

We all looked at her aghast and she threw up her hands.

"What? I am old, not dead!" Rose turned to me. "You are still a handsome woman. A little uptight, but handsome."

"I'm not looking for another husband," I told the incorrigible old woman firmly.

"Then a lover?" She leaned forward conspiratorially. "Sex is very good for the complexion."

Grace choked on her wine, gasping for breath.

Henry was studying his plate like it held the secrets of the universe. His shoulders were shaking slightly. The bastard was laughing.

"I'll keep that in mind," I said flatly.

"You should! Look at me—eighty-four and my skin is beautiful!" Rose gestured at her face, which was indeed remarkably unlined for someone her age. "Good sex is the secret."

"I thought butter was the secret," I pointed out.

Begonia burst out laughing, nearly knocking over her wine glass. "Oh, Helena! You've got her there. You are quick!"

"Years of dealing with politicians. You learn to think on your feet."

"Or run away very fast," Henry muttered into his wine.

"That too."

The evening stretched on, the food disappearing, the wine flowing, the conversation meandering from topic to topic with the easy randomness of people who were just beginning to know each other. In the distance, the distinct wail of a French emergency siren echoed. Through it all, Begonia presided like a benevolent queen, making sure glasses stayed full and plates never emptied, steering the conversation away from awkward silences and toward laughter.

"You are good at this," I observed during a lull.

"At what?"

"This." I gestured around the table. "Bringing people together. Making them comfortable."

"Ah, this is easy. People want to be comfortable, to be welcome. You simply give them what they want." She leaned closer, lowering her voice. "And if they are difficult, you give them wine until they are too drunk to be difficult."

"That explains a lot about French foreign policy."

She threw her head back and laughed, the sound carrying across the terrace and out into the darkening fields beyond.

The temperature had dropped as the evening wore on, the dancing flames in the chimineas on either end of the terrace were working overtime to keep the chill at bay. Grace had wrapped herself in her cardigan, and the German couple had moved their chairs closer to the nearest heater. But no one seemed inclined to leave, the spell of the evening holding everyone in place.

"This is nice," I said, surprising myself with the admission.

Begonia smiled, reaching over to pat my hand. "Yes, *chérie*. This is nice. And tomorrow will be nice. And the day after that. You will see. France, she knows how to heal a broken heart."

"My heart's not broken," I said automatically.

"No?" She raised an eyebrow.

I opened my mouth to deny it, to deflect with humor or sarcasm or one of the hundred other defense mechanisms I'd perfected over the years. But sitting there, under the fairy lights, with wine warming my blood and the sound of laughter surrounding me, I found I didn't have the energy.

"Maybe it's a little broken," I admitted.

"Then we will fix it. With wine and cheese and butter."
She smiled. "And perhaps we will unbutton that top button, yes?"

"Don't push your luck."

"I always do, *chérie*. I always do."

7

Sunday Morning

The next time I woke up, there was pale sunlight filtering through the linen curtains and the distant sound of a rooster losing its mind. I rolled out of bed and brushed my teeth, squinting against the bright bathroom lighting. It wasn't quite a hangover, but I was definitely feeling the effects of the last few days. I needed coffee and some fresh air. I could knock on Henry and Grace's doors. We could have breakfast together, maybe take a walk around the garden.

Or I could slip downstairs alone like the coward I was.

"Coward it is," I announced to the empty bathroom.

Decision made, I dressed quickly in pleated khakis and my favorite sweater set, before carefully poking my head into the hallway. Henry's door remained firmly closed, no sound from within. Good. I'd face him after I'd built up my courage with breakfast and caffeine.

The stairs creaked under my feet despite my attempts at stealth but no one stirred. The scent of fresh bread and brewing coffee grew stronger as I descended.

Rose was in the lobby, arranging a vase of fresh flowers on the countertop. She looked up as I entered and frowned.

"You are awake early, Madame Barrett."

"I had a nice long nap yesterday," I said with a smile. "And please, call me Helena." I cocked my head. "Is that coffee I smell?"

Rose waved a hand toward the archway to the left. "It is in the kitchen," she said. "Help yourself."

The kitchen was bright and airy, with high ceilings and gorgeous wood cabinets, their finish golden in the sunlight. Begonia leaned against the counter, looking bright-eyed and bushy-tailed for this early hour of the morning. She was wrapped in a long knitted shawl, her hands cradling a delicate white ceramic mug.

She gave me a considering look. "Look who is up and about with the roosters."

"I was thinking about exploring your lovely garden," I said, waving an arm toward the door. "But first I wanted to beg a cup of that delicious smelling coffee."

"Of course, *mon cher*." Begonia set down her own cup and poured one for me. "Come with me to the village. I will show you the little market there. Gaspard will have fish this morning and I need something for tonight's dinner." She leaned in conspiratorially. "Between us, his fish is the best in the region, but we can never tell him, for he will raise his prices."

"I wouldn't want to intrude—"

"Nonsense! It will be fun, yes?" She waggled her eyebrows.

Resistance was clearly futile. Within minutes we were outside, the air at that pleasant threshold between cool and comfortable that was perfect for a brisk walk. Begonia led the way, a large wicker basket draped over one arm.

The big white cat was sprawled on the front steps again, his enormous body blocking the path like a furry speedbump. He fixed me with his golden stare, his tail swishing once in what I chose to interpret as acknowledgment rather than judgment. A stuttering purr roared to life.

"He likes you," Begonia declared.

"He does not. He hissed at me yesterday," I told her.

"There you go." She shrugged, carefully picking her way around the beast.

"So!" Begonia said brightly, as we walked through the gates. "Tell me about your man."

"John? He's been gone two years now."

"Pah! Not your husband. He is the past. Tell me about Monsieur O'Connell."

My face heated and I nearly tripped on the uneven lane. "Henry is not my man." I looked around us desperately for something to change the subject. "Oh! Are those figs?"

Begonia gave me a knowing side eye, but took the bait. "Shall we pick some on our way back? Rose makes a lovely pudding."

We were about a quarter mile from the inn at this point and I looked up and down the road. "Don't they belong to someone?"

Begonia's laugh rang out like a bell in the early morning air. "Do not worry, *mon cher*, no one will care if we take a few."

Eventually the roughly tarmacked road beneath our feet transitioned to cobblestones and the village appeared ahead. It consisted of perhaps a dozen cross streets off the main road, each one a narrow path winding between hous-es with shuttered windows and flower boxes. One block over from the main thoroughfare, a fountain burbled in the town square, surrounded by a scattering of stalls selling everything from vegetables to cheese to underwear.

"It is quiet today!" Begonia linked her arm through mine, pulling me toward the tiny market, She greeting what seemed like every person by name. We bought vegetables from a woman who sang as she weighed each item and cheese from a man with a magnificent mustache.

"I do not see Gaspard. Where is everyone this morning?" she asked, as the mustachioed man wrapped her purchases in thick white paper.

He shrugged. "No one knows." He nodded toward the other side of the square. "His shop is closed but he is not here. We are missing half our booths, as well. None of the vendors from Nice have arrived."

Begonia frowned. "Trouble on the road perhaps?"

Another Gallic shrug, this one even deeper. "Louisa thinks it is this flu that they are talking about on the news. She went to see her cousin in the city on Friday, who was quite ill and in a bad temper with it."

"Oh, *putain de merde!*" Begonia bit out, throwing her hands wide. "Not that again." She turned to me, tucking my hand back into her elbow. "Come, Helena. Let's go back to the inn before one of these bastards breathes on us."

The cheese man laughed, waving us off. As Begonia and I stepped out from under the canopy of his stall, the air displacement of a fast moving object pushed us aside like a missile. It impacted into the table, sending cheese flying everywhere and for a long moment, my feet lost the ground.

My ass found it.

"Helena!" Begonia's face swam into view above me, her expression wild. "Are you hurt?"

"I'm okay," I answered automatically, letting her pull me to my feet. Only then did I do a physical inventory. My tailbone throbbed. My palms stung where I'd caught myself on the cobblestones. But everything seemed to be in working order.

"I'm okay," I repeated, with more confidence. "What happened?"

French words, angry and rapid-fire, were coming from somewhere to my right. Hanging onto Begonia's hands for balance, I turned to see a pile of sticks where the cheese stall once stood.

In the middle of the destruction, a man wearing bright yellow spandex was climbing to his feet, a line of blood crossing his forehead as he threw what seemed to be random insults. His knees were a mess and one arm hung limply, but otherwise the man was upright and ambulatory.

Which was more than could be said for the cheese man's stall. The table and display were completely demolished and the canopy had half collapsed, one pole bent at an unnatural angle. Wheels of cheese had scattered across the cobblestones like enormous hockey pucks. An actual metal wheel spun lazily in the center of the mess and it took my rattled brain long moments to process that it had been part of a bicycle.

That explained the man's outfit, more pieces clicking into place. There were so few occasions for skintight yellow spandex, unfortunately. Despite the blood, the cyclist was still screaming, but his attention was now directed at the cheese seller, who was attempting to climb to his feet.

Once upright, the merchant screamed back, his magnificent mustache quivering with rage. Their French was too fast for me to follow, but I did pick up a few choice words.

All around us, people were gathering, a crowd forming in a loose circle. But nobody moved to intervene. They just stood there, watching, mouths hanging open in shock.

The cyclist paused in his diatribe to take a breath and I reached out a hand to get his attention.

"Are you okay? *Avez-vous besoin d'un hôpital?*" My voice was wobblier than I expected, but I didn't think I butchered the pronunciation too badly.

The cyclist turned his red-rimmed eyes to me and lunged.

I stepped back, my body moving before my brain could catch up, and Henry appeared from nowhere and inserted himself between us. He had one hand on the cyclist's chest, holding him back with what looked like minimal effort. The other hand was raised toward the cheese seller in a universal gesture for calm.

"Easy," Henry said, his voice carrying that particular quality of command that tolerated no argument. "Everyone just—"

The cheese man plopped down onto the ground, cradling his head. The adrenaline that had been fueling his side of the fight completely extinguished. The cyclist, however, must have had a death wish. He shoved against Henry's hand, eyes red and wild.

Henry's expression hardened. His hand shifted, gripping the front of the cyclist's jersey, and suddenly the man was facedown on the ground, his arms held in place behind his back, where Henry sat talking to him in calm tones that I couldn't hear over the ringing in my ears.

By the time the big yellow and red ambulance pulled up, Henry had given up trying to talk to the cyclist, who still thrashed and spat under him. The little crowd we'd attracted had all wandered off and most of the vendors were starting to pack up as well.

Begonia and I sat on the fountain's edge and watched two very tired looking EMTs wrestle the cyclist onto a stretcher. Within a few minutes he was strapped down, and wheeled away.

Henry dusted himself off and walked over to us, his face grim. "Are you sure you aren't hurt?"

"Just my pride," I answered, as Begonia and I stood.

He gave me a once over and nodded. "Let's get out of here."

He didn't have to ask twice. The three of us hurried back down the narrow street, our footsteps echoing off the stone buildings that pressed close on either side. The air here was cooler, shaded, carrying the damp smell of old stone and moss.

We encountered no one on our way back to the inn. The morning sun was still shining through the trees that lined the road. The birds still sang. Somewhere in the distance, a rooster crowed.

"The guy on the bike," I said, breaking the silence. "Do you think he was on something?"

Henry's expression darkened. "It seems likely."

"No, no," Begonia said firmly. "Not Maurice."

"Maurice was the man in yellow?" I clarified. "You know him?"

She nodded emphatically. "For many years," she replied. "Maurice is the local doctor in the village. He rides his bike and does not smoke. He would never do drugs." She shook her head and shrugged, her eyebrows pulling together. "And he would never deliberately damage his very expensive bike."

Begonia paused for a moment to look back over her shoulder at the village, small in the distance. "It does not make sense," she muttered, before walking on.

We traveled the rest of the way in silence. The inn appeared ahead, its honey-colored stone warm in the sunlight, geraniums bright in their window boxes. The cat was still sprawled on the front steps, a monument to feline indifference.

Begonia stepped over the beast, who didn't move. "We have guests departing this morning, so I must leave you, *mes chers.*"

She swept past us into the inn, leaving me and Henry standing in the courtyard. The cat opened one eye, assessed us, and apparently decided we weren't interesting enough to warrant his attention.

"Helena—"

"I'll see you at dinner," I said, moving toward the door before he could respond. I left him standing in the courtyard, each step an effort. My hands were throbbing now, the adrenaline wearing off and leaving pain in its wake. My ass was going to be purple by tomorrow.

Good thing there was no one to see it.

8

Sunday Afternoon

Ashley

"Still no signal?" Ashley asked, keeping her eyes on the road. She'd had to pee for the last two hours.

"No." He jabbed at the screen with his thumb, his movements getting sharper with each attempt. "This is ridiculous. I'm paying through the nose for international service."

An exit appeared on the right and Ashley flicked on the turn signal, earning an irritated honk from the car behind them.

"Jesus, these French drivers are aggressive," Robert muttered.

They pulled off the highway onto a smaller road that wound through fields of flowers. In different circumstances, Ashley would have found it beautiful. Now she just needed a bathroom and maybe some food that wasn't airline peanuts. They'd been on the road for nearly six hours and every place they'd tried to stop had been closed. The French really took their holidays seriously.

"There," Robert pointed ahead. "Gas station."

The station appeared like a mirage: a small building with two ancient-looking pumps out front. The sign advertising the price per liter was hand-painted, the numbers faded. Ashley pulled in, relieved to be off the highway even for a few minutes.

"Oh, thank god," she sighed.

The pumps were the old-fashioned kind with actual mechanical counters that spun as the gas flowed. Ashley fumbled with the nozzle, finally getting it into the tank.

"I'm going inside," Robert announced.

"Wait—" Ashley called after him, but he was already through the door.

She squeezed the handle, watching the numbers climb. Her feet ached in the Louboutins and she shifted her weight, trying to find a position that didn't aggravate her toes or her bladder.

The pump clicked off and Ashley replaced the nozzle and turned toward the station.

The building was small and dingy, the windows streaked with dirt. A bell chimed as she pushed open the door. Inside, it smelled like old coffee and something else—something sour and unpleasant that made her nose wrinkle.

Robert stood at the counter, his posture rigid. On the other side, a man with thinning hair and a stained shirt was staring at him, his face twisted in disgust.

"The card reader is broken," Robert said without turning around. "Do you have euros?"

"Yes." Ashley dug through her purse. She had made sure to exchange money before leaving home. "How much do you need?"

The man behind the counter spoke, his voice raspy and harsh. The tone was hostile, accusatory.

"I don't speak French," Robert said loudly, as if volume would solve the language barrier. "The. Card. Reader. Is. Broken."

The man erupted in another stream of French, his voice rising with each word. He gestured wildly, his movements jerky and uncoordinated. Spittle flew from his lips.

Robert took a step back, his hand moving to Ashley's shoulder. "We're leaving," he announced.

The man reached across the counter, his fingers grasping.

Gasping, Ashley threw two fifty euro bills at him and stepped backward, into Robert.

"Let's get out of here." Robert's hand tightened on her shoulder, shoving her toward the door.

They stumbled outside, the bell chiming cheerfully above them. Ashley's heart was hammering against her ribs. The man continued shouting, his voice following them. The words were incomprehensible but the rage was crystal clear.

"Get in the car," Robert ordered, already moving to the passenger side. "Now."

Ashley's hands shook as she fumbled with the door handle. Behind them, the station door slammed open. She didn't look back, just threw herself into the driver's seat and jammed the key into the ignition.

The engine roared to life and Ashley threw the car into gear, nearly clipping the pump as the car shot forward, throwing them both back against their seats. Ashley's pulse was racing, her breath coming in short gasps. In the rearview mirror, the attendant stood in the middle of the road, still shouting, his arms raised above his head.

"What the hell was that?" she gasped.

"Crazy, that's what." Robert was twisted in his seat, looking back. "Completely unhinged. Did you see his eyes? The guy was clearly on something."

"I hope that was enough to cover the gas," Ashley ventured.

"Well, if not he can take it up with his manager." Robert pulled out his phone again, jabbing at it. "Still no signal. This is ridiculous."

They drove in silence for a while, the countryside rolling past in shades of green and gold. Back on the main road, there were few cars and the driving was easy. On a long straight stretch of highway, a plume of smoke rose up ahead and Ashley began to slow the car.

Robert looked up from his phone and stared ahead, his mouth hanging open.

Multiple cars had collided in front of the exit, one on its side, another spun sideways across both lanes. Glass glittered on the pavement like scattered diamonds.

"Oh my god," Ashley breathed.

One car's door hung open. A woman was slumped against the steering wheel, her blonde hair obscuring her face. In the other car, someone was moving—jerky, uncoordinated movements that made Ashley's stomach turn over.

"We should stop," she said, already looking for a place to pull over. "They might need help."

"Keep driving." Robert's voice was flat.

"But—"

"I said keep driving, Ashley."

She hesitated, her foot hovering between the brake and gas. In the wrecked car, the person was slamming against the window. Their face pressed against the glass, mouth open in what might have been a scream or a snarl.

"Ashley. Drive. Now."

The sharp command in his voice snapped her out of her paralysis. She guided the car around the wreckage, her hands trembling again. In the distance, she could hear sirens—high and wavering, growing closer.

"Help is coming," she said, mostly to herself.

"Great. Not our problem."

Ashley's hands tightened on the wheel. "People could be dying back there. I think that person was having a seizure."

"I'm not a doctor and neither are you. Getting involved would accomplish what, exactly?" Robert didn't look up from his phone. "All we'd do is get in the way."

"We could have called for help or something."

"You heard the sirens. Someone already called. What were you planning to do, hold the woman's hand while we waited? Give the guy in the other car a pep talk?" His voice dripped with sarcasm. "Use your head, Ash."

The nickname that usually made her feel warm and special now just made her feel small.

"I just think—"

"That's your problem. You think with your heart instead of your brain." He finally looked up, his expression somewhere between exasperated and condescending. "Look, I get it. You want to help. It's sweet. But sometimes the smart thing is to keep your head down and focus on your own situation."

Ashley swallowed the lump in her throat. He was probably right. He usually was. He'd built a successful company from nothing, made himself a fortune, navigated boardrooms and business deals that made her head spin.

"You're right," she said quietly. "Sorry."

"Don't apologize." He reached over, patting her knee. "You'll learn."

Ashley nodded, her lips pressed together.

"So," Robert said, settling back in his seat. "How much further to this hotel?"

"Um." Ashley glanced at the map. "I don't know. That was our exit."

"What?"

"That was our turn." Ashley shrugged.

"Fuck. Fine. We're skipping it." He nodded to himself. "I'm making an executive decision."

"Skipping it?" Ashley asked blankly.

Robert had already turned back to his phone and waved a hand in her direction. "Just take us right to the inn that you booked for the rest of the week. The Maison something?"

"La Maison des Fleurs," Ashley said automatically. Her mind was still catching up. "But our reservation doesn't start until tomorrow."

"I'm sure they'll make room for us."

"But what if they're full?"

"Then we'll pay them to not be full." He scoffed. He turned to look out the window, his jaw tight. "I thought you wanted me to be more spontaneous. Romantic."

"I'm just trying to—"

"Trying to control everything instead of going with the flow." He turned back to her, his expression softening slightly in a way that somehow made her feel worse. "Look, I know you put a lot of work into planning this. And I appreciate it, I really do. But sometimes you need to be able to adapt. Roll with the punches. That's life in the real world."

Ashley's throat felt tight. "I just wanted everything to be perfect."

"And it will be. Once we get to this inn and can actually relax." He reached over, squeezing her knee again. "Come on, Ash. Don't pout. It's not a good look on you."

She wasn't pouting. She was trying not to cry. But she nodded anyway, keeping her eyes on the road.

"Good girl." He pulled his hand back. "Wake me when we get close."

And just like that, he leaned his seat back and closed his eyes, leaving Ashley alone with her thoughts and the endless gray highway stretching ahead.

And I still have to pee, Ashley thought sadly.

98

9

Sunday Evening

Helena

There was a distant bang and I jolted awake, my heart hammering against my ribs. For a moment I thought I was back in the White House, where late night emergencies weren't uncommon.

But I was alone in the bed and the pillows were lavender-scented.

"What the hell?" I muttered, sitting up.

My door flew open before I could get out of bed. Henry stood in the hallway, already dressed, which was both impressive and deeply annoying.

"Stay here," he commanded, and swung the door shut again.

"Like hell," I said to the empty room. I swung my legs out of bed, grateful I'd had the foresight to wear actual pajamas. "This is my vacation. If someone's going to ruin it at three in the morning, I'm going to know why."

I grabbed my cardigan and made it out of the room in time to see Henry disappear down the stairs. I followed.

The lobby was ablaze with light, the chandelier overhead glittering like it was hosting a state dinner. Begonia stood near the front desk in a silk robe the color of peacock feathers, her hair a red cloud around her head. Jean Luc hovered beside her in a pair of hastily pulled on jeans, his surprisingly sculpted chest bare.

Facing off with Begonia was a man in his early fifties, wearing a rumpled blazer over designer jeans. His face was red, his unnaturally dark hair plastered to his forehead with sweat as he stood with his hands on his hips.

"—absolutely unacceptable," he was saying, his voice carrying that particular pitch of entitlement that made my teeth ache. "We have a reservation. We paid in advance. I don't care what time it is—"

"*Monsieur*," Begonia began, her voice strained in a way I hadn't heard before, "I understand your frustration, but as I have explained, your check-in time is at four in the afternoon. Tomorrow."

"Do I look like I can wait until tomorrow?" He jabbed a finger at her, and Henry's shoulders tensed.

The young woman beside him had dark circles under her eyes, but forced a smile. "I'm so sorry about this," she told Begonia. "Robert," she said quietly, touching his arm. "Maybe we should—"

"I've got this, Ashley." He shook her off without looking at her. "As I was saying, we need a room. Now. I'll pay double. Triple. Whatever it takes."

Begonia's expression had shifted from irritation to something harder. "*Monsieur*, I am sympathetic to your situation, but I cannot simply conjure—"

"*Maman*," Jean Luc interrupted softly. He'd moved closer to Ashley, I noticed, and was looking at her with concern. "We do have the Rose Suite empty."

"That suite is not prepared," Begonia said sharply. "The linens need changing, the room needs—"

"I can change the linens." Jean Luc straightened his shoulders. "It will take ten minutes."

He turned to run up the stairs and caught himself short at the sight of Henry and me standing there in our pajamas. "Madame Barrett! I'm so sorry this commotion has disturbed your sleep."

I stepped out of his way and shook my head. "Not *your* fault, Jean Luc."

With a nod he slipped past me and hustled up the stairs, no doubt eager to get out of the line of fire.

Across the lobby Robert's eyes narrowed as he took me in—rumpled pajamas, no makeup, hair probably resembling a bird's nest. I could see him cataloging, dismissing, preparing to ignore me.

"I don't know who you are—" he began.

"Madame Barrett is our honored guest," Begonia interjected, her chin lifting. "She was the First Lady of your own country. You should show respect."

Oh Christ. There went any hope of anonymity.

Ashley's hand flew to her mouth. "Oh my god. Mrs. Barrett? I voted for your husband. Twice." Her eyes welled up. "I'm so sorry for your loss."

"Thank you," I said automatically, the words worn smooth by repetition. Then, because she looked like she might actually start crying, "It's Helena, please. And you're Ashley?"

She nodded, then seemed to remember the man beside her. "This is Robert. Robert Kovak. He's my—" She hesitated, and in that pause I saw everything I needed to know about their relationship. "—my fiancé. And my boss."

Jesus Christ.

Henry made a sound that might have been a cough.

"Well," I said, managing not to let my thoughts show on my face. Years of political training had to be good for something. "Robert, Ashley. This is Henry, my chief of security. And I believe you've met our hostess, Begonia, and her son Jean Luc."

Robert was staring at me now, his expression shifting through several calculations. I could practically see him recalibrating his approach, deciding whether my presence here meant he should be more polite or whether he could leverage it somehow.

"Mrs. Barrett," he said, his voice smoothing out into something that probably worked on shareholders. "I apologize. It's been a difficult night. You understand."

"I understand you're tired." I glanced at Begonia, who was running a hand over her wild hair. "We all are."

Begonia's eyes flickered between Robert and me, then she sighed—a great, dramatic exhale that would have been funny under different circumstances. "Perhaps a snack while we wait? You must be hungry."

"We're fine," Robert said curtly.

"We're starving," Ashley corrected quietly. "Thank you. That would be amazing."

Begonia swept toward the kitchen, her peacock robe billowing behind her. Henry remained by my side, unnaturally still in that way he got when he was cataloging threats. I didn't think Robert was dangerous, exactly. Just an asshole. But I understood Henry's caution.

Ashley had collapsed into one of the lobby's overstuffed chairs, her eyes closing.

"What happened?" I asked, settling into the chair across from her.

Her eyes opened. "Nothing was open. We had reservations in Avignon. But there was a huge pileup on the highway and we missed our turn. Robert wanted to just drive straight through." She glanced at him—he'd moved to the front windows and was staring out into the darkness, phone still clutched in his hand. "It's been a really long day."

"A pileup?" Henry's voice was sharp.

Ashley nodded. "Multiple cars. Earlier we stopped at a gas station and the attendant completely lost it when Robert tried to pay with a card." Her hands were shaking. "It's like everyone here is going crazy."

Begonia returned with a tray bearing cheese, bread, and a bottle of cognac and three crystal tumblers. She set it on the small table between us and poured generous measures into each glass, pushing one toward Ashley.

"Doctor's orders," Begonia said firmly when Ashley started to protest.

"You're not a doctor," I pointed out, accepting my own glass.

"Details." Begonia waved a dismissive hand.

Jean Luc galloped down the stairs, slightly out of breath, now sporting a plain white shirt over his jeans. He stopped on the bottom step. "Your room is ready. If you would follow me?"

Ashley was on her feet immediately, swaying slightly. "Thank you again," she said with a tired smile. "I'm so sorry about all this."

She followed Jean Luc back up the stairs, a sullen Robert in her wake.

As soon as they disappeared up the stairs, Begonia let out a sound that was half laugh, half groan and tossed back the rest of her cognac. "*Mon Dieu*. What a tool."

"That was kind of Jean Luc," I said.

"My son has a soft heart. Like his father." Begonia refilled her glass. "That poor girl."

"I noticed."

"Terrible." Begonia shook her head. "Young women these days. They think money is romance."

"Young women have always thought that," I said. "And older men have always exploited it."

Henry cleared his throat. "We should all try to get some sleep."

"I'm going to stay down here for a bit," I announced.

Henry's expression said exactly what he thought of that idea.

"You can join us, *cher*," Begonia offered with a sly smile. "We will drink cognac and talk about romance. It is a very French tradition."

"I'm going to bed," Henry said flatly. But he hesitated, looking at me. "Helena—"

"I'm fine. Go."

A battle played out across Henry's face, and exhaustion won out. He nodded and headed back upstairs, his footsteps heavy on the wooden treads.

Begonia watched him go, then turned to me with raised eyebrows. "Are you sure he isn't your lover?"

I choked on my cognac. "Absolutely. Yes."

"Helena, *chérie*, I am French. I know these things. The way he looks at you—"

"He looks at me like I'm a security risk. Which, to be fair, I am." I set down my glass.

"If you say so." Begonia's smile was knowing. "But I think perhaps you are missing an opportunity."

"I think *perhaps* you should mind your own business."

"What fun would that be?" She refilled my glass without asking. "Your husband, he has been gone two years, yes?"

"Yes."

"It is time to think about living again, *mon ami*."

"I am living." I waved a hand regally to encompass the entirety of the lobby. "I'm on vacation."

"You are running," Begonia corrected gently. "But you cannot run forever."

"Watch me."

She laughed, that rich, warm sound I was beginning to associate with her. "You are very stubborn. I like this about you." She raised her glass. "To stubborn women."

I clinked my glass against hers. "To stubborn women. And unsolicited relationship advice."

"Santé!"

10

Monday Morning

The sunlight stabbing through the curtains felt personal, like the universe had decided I needed to be punished for my sins. I cracked one eye open and immediately regretted it.

"Fuck," I whispered to the empty room.

My mouth tasted like something had died in it. Something that had been marinating in cognac. The clock on the nightstand swam into focus: 9:47 AM. I'd missed breakfast. Also, apparently, my common sense.

The full weight of last night's decisions settled over me like a wet blanket. Begonia and I had polished off that entire bottle of cognac. At some point we'd moved to the kitchen, where we'd made cheese toast and discussed the varying degrees of male stupidity across multiple continents.

It had been, objectively, a terrible idea.

It had also been the most fun I'd had in years. Possibly decades, no offense to John.

I dragged myself upright, my head protesting the movement with a dull throb that promised to get worse before it got better. The bathroom mirror confirmed what I already knew: I looked like shit. My hair had achieved a gravity-defying angle that would have impressed Einstein, and there were pillow creases on my pale face deep enough to plant crops in.

"You are old," I told my reflection. "This is what an old person looks like after a night of drinking."

I brushed my teeth twice, ran a comb through my hair without much hope of improvement, and pulled on a pair of comfortable trousers and a soft sweater. My palms were still scraped from yesterday's bicycle incident, the abraded skin pink and tender.

The hallway was mercifully quiet. I made it three steps before Grace's door popped opened.

"Helena! I'm so glad you're up!" She was entirely too chipper for whatever ungodly hour this was. "I thought you were going to sleep all day!"

"I considered it," I admitted.

Grace was dressed for an outing—pressed pants, a cute blouse, her hair perfectly styled. She looked fresh and rested and offensively young.

"The car for the perfume museum tour should be here in ten minutes," she said, consulting her phone. "You have time to grab a quick breakfast if you hurry!"

The thought of getting into a car and being driven anywhere, let alone to a museum where I'd be expected to smell things, made my stomach lurch.

"I'm going to pass," I said.

"But you were so excited about it when we booked it!"

Had I been? That seemed unlikely. Then again, I'd also thought drinking an entire bottle of cognac was a good idea, so my judgment was clearly questionable.

"I'm taking it easy today," I said firmly. "Besides, you'll have more fun without me."

Grace's face fell, but she rallied quickly. "Are you sure? I don't mind staying—"

"Grace. Go. Smell the perfumes. Take pictures. Live your best life." I patted her shoulder. "I'll be fine."

"Well, if you're sure..." She bit her lip. "Oh! I almost forgot. Begonia mentioned we were expecting an American couple today."

"They showed up in the middle of the night," I said. "Made quite an entrance. Apparently there was an accident out on the highway and they had to detour from their original hotel."

"That's awful." Grace checked her phone again. "I should probably go wait downstairs. The driver will be here soon."

I watched her practically skip down the hallway, her enthusiasm a crime against humanity. The stairs were a challenge, but I managed them without incident. Each step sent a small shockwave through my skull, a reminder that I was, in fact, too old for this shit.

The lobby was blessedly quiet, although the light streaming through the windows was entirely too bright. I squinted against it, making my way toward what I hoped would be coffee.

Rose intercepted me in the archway to the kitchen.

"Good morning, sunshine," she said, her voice dripping with judgment.

I'd faced down hostile foreign dignitaries, Congressional committees, and a press corps that could smell blood in the water from a mile away. I could handle one tiny French octogenarian. Probably.

"Good morning, Rose."

Her sharp eyes traveled over me, taking in my rumpled appearance, the faint tremor in my hands, the way I was squinting against the light like a vampire at dawn.

"You were up late," she observed.

"Was I?"

Rose's mouth pursed. "Begonia is a bad influence."

"It was mutual." I spotted the coffee pot on the countertop and made my way toward it like a woman crossing a desert toward an oasis. "Besides, we're both adults."

"And old enough to know better." Rose followed me, her tiny frame somehow managing to loom. "You drank all the good cognac."

"Put it on my tab."

"That cognac was from 1972."

I paused, the coffee pot halfway to my cup. "Seriously?"

"Seriously."

"Shit."

"Exactly." But Rose's expression had softened slightly, a hint of amusement creeping into her eyes. "Although, between you and me, I think Begonia has been saving it for too long. My son would have wanted it to be enjoyed."

I finished pouring, the smell of coffee making my stomach settle slightly. "Your son had good taste."

"He married Begonia." Rose's eyes twinkled as she shrugged and I couldn't tell if she was agreeing or submitting evidence to the contrary. "Come, sit. I will make you toast. It will help."

I followed her to the small table by the window, the sunlight slightly less offensive from this angle. Within minutes Rose produced a stack of perfectly golden slices of toast, butter already melting into each surface.

"Eat," she commanded.

I ate. The toast was as good as it looked—crispy on the outside, soft on the inside, the butter adding just enough richness to settle my protesting stomach. I was halfway through the second piece when Begonia swept into the room.

She looked absolutely radiant.

That bitch.

"Helena!" She beamed at me, her caftan today a swirl of blues and greens that made her look like a walking Monet painting. "You are awake! How do you feel?"

"Like death."

"Excellent! Me too!" She collapsed into the chair across from me, stealing a piece of my toast. "We had such fun last night, yes?"

"I can feel my heartbeat in my eyeballs."

Begonia threw her head back and laughed, the sound filling the small dining room. "You Americans. So dramatic."

"Look who's talking."

Rose materialized beside us with a tray bearing a coffee pot and what looked like fresh pastries. She set it down with more force than strictly necessary.

"You two are children," she announced. "Drinking and staying up all night. Shameful."

Begonia dissolved into giggles, and I found myself joining her. It was stupid and childish and my head was pounding, but God, it felt good.

"You are both impossible," Rose declared, but she was definitely smiling now. She turned and swept out of the room, her small frame managing to convey deep disapproval and grudging affection in equal measure.

Henry appeared in the archway, his hair still damp from a shower, dressed in dark jeans and a plain blue shirt. He stopped short at the sight of us, his expression shifting through several emotions in rapid succession: confusion, concern, and then something that looked like relief.

"You're laughing," he said, his voice carrying a note of wonder that would have been funny under different circumstances.

"Occasionally I do that," I said. "I'm a human being with a full range of emotions."

"I was starting to wonder." But his mouth was quirking upwards at the corner. He pulled out a chair and sat down, his movements easy. "Good to see you relaxing."

"Begonia is a terrible influence."

"The best kind." Henry helped himself to coffee, his eyes cataloging the scene before him—the crumb-covered plates, Begonia's theatrical outfit, my rumpled state. "I was going to yell at you for ditching the museum tour with Grace."

"I'm taking a personal day."

"You're taking a vacation from your vacation?"

"It's been kind of a stressful vacation so far."

Begonia leaned forward, her bangles chiming. "Henry, you should go with Grace! She should not go alone."

"Absolutely not." Henry's response was immediate and firm. "I'm not leaving Helena."

"I'm perfectly safe here," I protested.

"You nearly got run over yesterday."

"I got knocked on my ass. There's a difference."

Begonia was watching us with undisguised delight, her head swiveling back and forth like she was at a tennis match. "You two bicker like an old married couple."

"We do not," Henry and I said simultaneously, then turned to frown at each other.

"See?" Begonia gestured at us triumphantly. "*Adorable!*"

I stood up, my chair scraping against the floor. "I'm going for a walk."

"I'm coming with you," Henry said, already on his feet.

"You aren't invited."

Begonia's laughter followed us out of the kitchen and across the lobby. Ignoring Henry, I swung open the front door of the inn and stepped outside as the herd of tiny goats rounded the front of the house. They bleated at my interruption as they continued toward the field on the right where they split into two groups to flow around a wooden bench beneath a tree at the edge of the gravel.

Grace sat on the bench, her face buried in a book, absently stroking the fat white cat draped across her lap. She looked up as the goats swarmed her, delighted by their antics.

I followed in the herd's wake and Grace gave a little wave as she looked up.

"Helena! I thought you were resting?"

"I tried. Henry's harassing me." I settled onto the bench beside her, Henry unrepentantly taking up a position a few feet away where he could keep an eye on us, the goats, and the road beyond the gate. "Shouldn't your car have been here by now?"

She slipped a pretty floral bookmark into the pages and closed the book, a gothic romance with an embossed dust jacket and sprayed edges. "I wasn't paying attention. What time is it?" She pulled her phone out of her bag. "Oh, wow. They're really late."

"Traffic, probably," I said, remembering Ashley's story about blocked roads and accidents. "You should give them a call."

She tapped at her phone, frowning at the screen. "That's weird."

"What?"

"No signal." She held up her phone, showing me the lack of bars. "I had five bars when I sat down here. Now nothing."

"Does the wifi reach out here?"

Grace jabbed at her screen. "I'm connected to the wifi, but no internet. No cell service. Nothing." She looked up, her expression shifting from confused to worried. "Is yours working?"

"I left mine in my room," I shrugged.

"Could be a tower issue," Henry said. "Or solar flares. That can interfere with signals."

Grace checked her phone again, as if the signal might have magically reappeared in the last ten seconds. "This is so frustrating. I was really looking forward to this tour." She slumped back against the bench, dislodging the cat, who stalked off in a huff. "Did you know the museum has a perfume bottle that's over four thousand years old? And I signed up for the workshop where you create your own scent."

"That sounds really interesting," I offered lamely.

"You're just saying that to make me feel better."

"Is it working?"

"Not really, but I appreciate the thought."

We sat there for another few minutes, Grace periodically checking her phone with increasing frustration. Movement caught my eye at the bend in the road to the village and I leapt to my feet only to immediately sag.

"It's just a person walking," I dismissed.

Grace glanced up and returned to her phone but Henry frowned at the distant figure. They shuffled unevenly along the road toward the inn for a few yards before turning abruptly into one of the fields and disappearing from view.

"Must be a farmer," I speculated.

"A drunk farmer," Henry added before turning to arch a brow at me. "There's a lot of that going around lately."

I shrugged. "Maybe it's catching." I turned to look down at Grace. "I don't think they're coming, hon. Can I interest you in a walk through the gardens instead?"

"You're feeling better?"

"I am," I said firmly. "Maybe there's something to this fresh air crap after all."

11

Monday Afternoon

Darla

Diesel and burnt rubber stung Darla's nose and she struggled to open her eyes.

"Mommy!" William's face appeared above her, his curls dark and wild in the dim light, his cheeks streaked with tears and dirt. "Mommy, wake up!"

"William?" Her voice came out as a croak. She tried to move and pain exploded across her ribs, white-hot and stunning. Taking a deep breath, Darla braced her hands against the smooth leather of the car seat and pushed herself up. The world was upside down.

No, it was the car that was upside down.

Darla stabbed at the button on her seatbelt and tumbled onto the roof of the car as her memory caught up to her.

They'd been trying to get away from the riots and the fires that had overtaken Nice. They'd lost contact with the rest of their security detail. Jacob had screamed at Dan to drive, just drive.

"Oh god." Darla whipped around to find William dangling beside the seat she'd just vacated. Her hands flew to his face, checking for injuries with shaking fingers. "Are you okay? Does anything hurt?"

"My straps are too tight." The words tumbled out in a rush. "Mommy, I want to go back to the hotel—"

"Shh, shh." She braced his body with her shoulder, despite the screaming protest of her ribs, and released his buckles. He tumbled into her arms. "It's okay. We're okay."

Except they very clearly weren't.

The rear window of the car was missing, the trunk crumpled like an accordion. Through the shattered glass, she could see other vehicles in similar shape. A white delivery van had run them off the road, the driver screaming as he came closer and closer. Dan's knuckles had been white against the steering wheel, then the world had begun spinning.

Moving carefully, Darla grabbed the back of the front seat and pulled herself forward. The windshield was gone, and so was Dan, but Jacob was slumped against the passenger door.

"Jacob?" Darla reached for him with one hand, keeping William pressed against her with the other. "Jacob, can you hear me?"

He didn't reply, but he was warm and his chest rose and fell.

Through the missing windshield, the asphalt stretched ahead at an odd angle. Darla closed her eyes for a moment, begging the world to stop spinning. When she opened them again, the world was right side up and Dan was climbing to his feet in the middle of the road.

"Dan!" Relief flooded through her. "Dan, Jacob's hurt—"

Dan turned toward them and Darla's words died in her throat.

His eyes were red-rimmed and streaming tears, his expression twisted into something feral and unfamiliar. Blood covered the front of his shirt. He moved toward them, one foot dragging behind him, his movements jerky and uncoordinated.

"Dan?" Darla tried again, her blood running cold.

Dan wrenched the passenger door open with enough force to tear it half off its remaining hinges. The screech of metal made William clap his hands over his ears and bury his face in Darla's shoulder.

Dan grabbed Jacob's arm and pulled. Jacob spilled from the car, tumbling out onto the road with a sickening thud. For a horrible moment he just lay there, his still face turned toward them and Darla's heart stuttered in her chest.

His eyes opened.

They were red, his pupils blown so wide his eyes looked black.

Jacob surged to his feet with an inhuman grace that sent ice flooding through Darla's veins. One moment he was crumpled on the ground, the next he was upright, swaying but on his feet.

"Jacob?" Her voice was barely a whisper.

He turned toward the sound but there was no recognition in his face. He took a step toward the car and was yanked backwards by Dan's hand on his shoulder. The two men went down in a tangle of limbs, rolling across the road in a mess of fists and grunts.

"Mommy, what's wrong with Daddy and Mr. Dan?" William's voice was small and terrified. "Why are they fighting?"

"We need to get out of the car." Darla's hands scrambled for the door handle. She found the lever and pulled, but the door didn't budge. She tried again, putting her shoulder into it despite the agony in her ribs. The door creaked but held. Shifting her weight back, she kicked at the door with both feet, pure adrenaline overriding the pain.

The door flew open with a shriek of tortured metal.

Darla crawled out onto the road, the pavement digging into her hands and knees. For a moment she just lay there, her vision swimming, her ribs on fire.

Get up, her brain commanded. Get up. Get up. Get up.

She got up.

The world tilted and spun but she stayed upright through sheer force of will. William scrambled out of the car behind her, his arms wrapping around her hips.

"We're okay," she told him. "We're okay—"

On the other side of the car, Jacob and Dan were still fighting. Dan had managed to knock Jacob to the ground and was leaning over him, his fist drawn back. He brought it down and the sound of the impact made Darla's stomach turn.

Jacob's head snapped to the side.

For a horrible moment, he was still. Then Jacob's eyes opened—those awful, wrong eyes—and he grabbed Dan's shirt and headbutted him with a crunch that echoed across the empty road.

Dan reeled backward, blood pouring from his nose, as Jacob climbed to his feet. They circled each other like animals. Dan's face was a mask of blood. Jacob's was twisted beyond recognition, all the warmth and kindness that made him her husband stripped away and replaced with something primitive and violent.

Darla's legs were moving before her brain caught up. She backed away, clutching William to her side. She took another step back. Then another. The road stretched out behind her, empty and silent except for the sounds of the fight and William's hiccupping sobs.

Run, her brain whispered. Run. Run. Run.

She ran.

Every step was agony. Her ribs ground together with each breath. Her head pounded. William stumbled and she lifted him into her arms and settled his weight onto her hip, swallowing back a cry of pain. She kept her eyes on the road ahead, on the tree line in the distance, on putting one foot in front of the other.

She walked for hours as the sun moved across the sky and sweat soaked through her blouse despite the chill in the air. In her arms, William stirred.

"Mommy, I need to pee."

Darla nodded. "Okay, honey. we'll find a place to stop soon."

"I need to pee now," he insisted, struggling to get down.

"William—"

"I'm gonna pee my pants!"

Darla set William down in a tangle of limbs, her arms screaming in relief. "Pee on this tree," she directed, gesturing toward a nice wide pine at the side of the road.

He scampered off, his earlier trauma apparently forgotten in the face of more immediate bodily needs. Darla sank to the grass behind him, burying her face in her hands.

Jacob. Oh god, Jacob.

"Mommy, I'm done!"

Darla wiped her eyes and held out her hand. "Good job, honey. Can you walk for a little while?"

"Where are we going?"

That was an excellent question. They'd fled inland from Nice with no destination in mind, just away from the chaos and violence. There was no cell service or internet. No GPS. Not that it mattered, since her phone had been in her purse, which was presumably still in the wreckage behind them.

"We're going to find help," she said with more confidence than she felt.

"What kind of help?"

"I don't know yet."

They walked. The road was deserted, not a single car passing in either direction. Trees pressed close on both sides, their leaves whispering as the afternoon turned breezy and cooler.

William had stopped asking questions after the first hour and lapsed into a tired silence that was somehow worse than his usual chatter.

The sun was beginning to set when Darla spotted the sign. It was small, wooden, half-hidden by overgrown vegetation. She almost missed it.

Saint-Amélie-de-Provence - 5 km

Saint-Amélie. The name tickled something in her memory. Where had she heard it before?

Darla's heart leaped.

"William." She squeezed his hand. "I know where we're going."

"Really?"

"Really." She started walking faster, pulling William along. Five kilometers.

They could do that.

12

Monday Evening

Helena

After our walk through the gardens, I spent the remainder of the day rotting in my room. I finished a mystery and started a memoir, reading in the bath and between long naps. I sat on my pretty little balcony watching bees navigate the lavender in the garden below.

As the sun dipped toward the horizon and painted the mountains in shades of gold and purple, I went back into the darkened room and crossed to turn on the frilly little lamp beside the bed.

Nothing happened.

The switch for the overhead light was similarly ineffective. A knock sounded at the door two inches from my shoulder and I nearly jumped out of my skin. I swung the door open and had the satisfaction of seeing the flicker of surprise that ran across Henry's face.

"What?" I asked aggressively, still recovering from the startle.

Henry recovered much faster than I did. "The power's out."

I sagged. "No shit, Sherlock." I waved toward the uncooperative light switch.

"Everything's out." He ran a hand through his hair, making it stand up in ways that were unfairly attractive. "No internet, no cell, no GPS. And now, no power."

"Maybe there's a pole down?" I suggested.

"Maybe."

"Let's go see if anyone knows what's going on." I skirted around Henry, who gave me just enough room to get by, and started down the stairs.

The lobby was empty, but a glow drew us to the courtyard. The fairy lights were dark, but the table was crowded with dozens of candles and the large terracotta chimineas were blazing at either end of the space. Grace was deep in conversation with our new arrivals at one end of the table. At the other, Begonia and Rose were having an animated argument while Jean Luc set out steaming trays of food.

"Helena!" Begonia cut Rose off mid sentence to greet me, a smile splitting her face. "The candlelight is so romantic, no?"

"I'm rather attached to the modern conveniences," I admitted sheepishly.

She patted my hand as I settled into the seat beside Grace. "No worries, *mon cher*. The *maison* has a *citerne de propane*. We can make good food and take long hot showers. What else could you possibly need?"

Grace leaned toward me and poured wine into my glass. "I need the internet," she muttered.

I squinted at her in the flickering light, recognizing the expression she wore when she was running on caffeine and nerves.

"Still nothing?" I asked.

She shook her head, two vertical creases forming between her eyebrows. "No cell, no internet."

"No shit," Robert said from the other side of the table. "Because apparently we're trapped in the fucking dark ages."

"Robert." Ashley said from beside him, her voice soft and placating. "Look at all of this wonderful food. Why don't you try the beef?"

"I don't want to try the fucking beef, Ashley. I want to check my email."

"We all want to check our email, Mr. Kovak," Henry said mildly, sinking into his chair on the opposite side of the table. "But the rest of us aren't whining about it."

Begonia clapped her hands. "*Mon dieu*, you all look like someone died. It is just the power, *mes amis*. It will come back."

"It's not just the power," Grace corrected quietly. "We haven't been able to get any news—"

"So we will have a quiet evening!" Begonia threw up her hands. "We eat, we drink, we tell stories by candlelight like people did for thousands of years before the invention of the smartphone. Where is your sense of adventure?"

Rose looked up from cutting the bread. "Adventure for those of us who don't need to call our families," she said pointedly.

"Your family is here, *chérie*."

"I was talking about the Americans."

Begonia shot her mother-in-law a look but didn't argue. She began passing around slices of the bread, a home-made boule, still warm, with butter that was probably hand-churned by some impossibly picturesque French maid, when a sound whispered through the darkness.

Footsteps on the gravel path. Slow, stumbling, uneven.

Henry was on his feet before I could blink. Everyone else had frozen, forks halfway to mouths, glasses suspended in mid-air.

The footsteps came closer. Then a woman's voice echoed into the stillness, thin and desperate: "Hello? I'm looking for Helena Barrett."

A familiar voice.

"Darla?" I pushed back from the table, nearly knocking over my chair.

A wavering form appeared behind one of the tall patio heaters, Illuminated by the flickering flames like something from a horror film. Filthy and tattered clothing hung from Darla's small frame and her face was streaked with dirt. She was limping, one arm wrapped around her mid-section, the other supporting a small figure pressed against her side.

William.

"Mon dieu!" Begonia sprang up, reaching Darla before me or Henry. She swept her soft purple shawl from her shoulders and wrapped it around them both. "What has happened?"

Darla's eyes found mine, a hand reaching out as I closed the distance between us. "Helena," she breathed, and then her knees buckled.

Henry caught her before she hit the ground, his movements smooth and practiced as he lowered them both to the terrace. "I've got you," he said quietly. "You're safe now."

Still holding Darla's hand, I dropped to my knees beside Henry, ignoring the protest of my bruised tailbone. Darla was conscious but barely, her eyes unfocused. Up close I could see the bruising on her face, the way she held her ribs, the scrapes covering her arms.

"Darla, what happened? Where's Jacob? Dan?"

Her eyes focused on mine and filled with tears. She shook her head once, sharp and definitive.

Ice flooded my veins. I looked up to find Henry's gaze on me, his expression grim.

William whimpered, pressing his face into his mother's shoulder. His curls were matted with dirt, his shirt torn at the collar. "I'm hungry."

I reached out, running a hand over the boy's hair. "Hey, William. It's Helena, do you remember me?"

He raised his head enough to peek out at me, giving me a very small nod.

"We have all kinds of good food right here. Would you like to sit next to my friend Grace and have some dinner?"

He gave me another small nod and Grace immediately appeared at my side, her expression warm and nonthreatening.

"Hi, William. It's so nice to meet you. Let's go sit at the table and I'll make you up a plate. How does that sound?"

William looked to his mother, who managed a nod. "Go with Miss Grace, honey. Mommy will be right there."

He went reluctantly, looking back over his shoulder every few steps. Once Grace had him installed at the table, Rose slid into the seat on his other side, her small frame radiating a fierce protectiveness.

Jean Luc reappeared with a suitcase-sized first aid kit and a purple velvet pillow that he eased under Darla's head.

"Where are you hurt?" Henry asked, cataloging her injuries the way he'd been trained to do.

"Ribs," Darla managed. "I think they're cracked. Every-thing else is just bruises, I think." She managed a weak laugh and I squeezed her hand.

Henry opened the kit and began pulling out supplies with practiced ease. "I need to check for a concussion. Can you follow my finger?"

Concussion ruled out, Henry eased Darla into a sitting position and began wrapping her ribs. While he worked, I tried to rub warmth into Darla's hand. It was ice cold despite the heaters. "We need to get her inside," I told Henry.

He nodded. "We can move her as soon as the ribs are stabilized." He paused to gently lift Darla's fringe and ex-amine the shallow cut at her hairline. "Then we need to clean these cuts. Can you tell us what happened?" he asked gently.

"There was an accident on the highway, the A8," she began quietly, her voice flat. "There were a lot of accidents, actually. Nice was a disaster. People were rioting, setting fires." She looked up, meeting my gaze. "People were just driving into the sides of buildings. It was crazy."

Henry's hands stilled. "Driving into buildings?"

"Like the cyclist." I was connecting the dots, too.

Darla continued, her hand tightening on mine. "Dan made the call to evacuate us out of the city. We were on our way to a safe house in Avignon, but the roads were crazy. We got separated from the rest of the team. People were just abandoning their cars and running down the highway."

She paused, a hand hovering over the wound on her forehead.

"A van ran our car off the road" she continued, her voice cracking. "The driver was screaming. Just screaming and screaming. Dan swerved but we hit the guardrail and flipped. When I woke up, the car was on its side and William was crying and Jacob—"

She stopped, her breathing coming faster.

"It's okay," I said softly.

Darla lifted her head, her gaze drilling into mine. "It's not, Helena. It's really not."

Henry had gone very still, a length of gauze forgotten in his hand.

"Dan kept saying he was hot," Darla continued. "Before the crash. He'd turned the air conditioning all the way up, took off his tie, then his jacket." She looked up at me, her eyes desperate. "Then after the crash, when he pulled Jacob out, his eyes were bloodshot. They both—"

Her voice broke entirely.

"You walked here?" Henry asked. His voice was calm but I could see the tension in his shoulders. "From Nice?"

"From where we crashed. I don't know how far. Miles. William was so brave." She looked toward the table, where her son was shoveling food into his mouth as if he'd been starving. "We saw the sign for Saint-Amélie and I remembered the name. I followed the road and just kept walking and hoping—"

"You did exactly the right thing," I told her firmly. "You're safe now. Both of you."

Begonia reappeared in the doorway. "The bed is made up in the Hibiscus room. Shall we move her there? I can bring up a tray of food."

"Yes, thank you." I looked at Darla. "Can you walk?"

She nodded, letting us help her to her feet. She swayed dangerously and Henry caught her elbow as William launched himself from the table, latching onto her side like a barnacle.

"It's okay, baby," Darla whispered, clutching him to her side. "I'm not going anywhere without you."

We followed Begonia inside and up the stairs at a glacial pace, Darla leaning heavily on both of us. The room was well lit with candles and the bed had been turned down and was ready, but Darla balked.

"I'm filthy," she protested. "May I use the bathroom?"

"Of course, *mon cher*," Begonia said gently. "I will get you something to change into." She disappeared in a flutter of fabric.

Darla leaned on me into the bathroom, but then stood up straight. "I've got this," she said firmly.

"I'll be on the other side of the door," I told her as I backed out of the room. "Just call if you need anything."

By the time the water turned off, Begonia had returned with a stack of clothing and disappeared again. I knocked gently at the door and passed through the items when it opened a crack.

A few minutes later, the door opened fully, revealing William dressed in an oversized man's t-shirt, yawning and rubbing his eyes, his hair in damp ringlets. Darla was right behind him, wearing another t-shirt and sweatpants, a towel wrapped around her hair. She herded William right to the bed, tucking him in and sitting beside him. The little boy closed his eyes and his body went slack as he immediately fell into sleep.

"It's been a long day," Darla said softly, stroking his hair away from his forehead.

"For both of you," I said gently. "Get some sleep. We can talk in the morning."

Darla's eyes filled again and she surged to her feet to wrap her arms around me. "Thank you. Thank you so much," she whispered into my shoulder before collapsing back on the bed.

I slipped out of the room quietly, closing the door behind me. In the hallway, Henry stood against the wall. I covered my mouth with my hand, swallowing down my own tears.

When I had collected myself, I met Henry's gaze. "Jacob—" I started. "What is going on, Henry?"

"Nothing good." He ran a hand through his hair again, making it stick up even more.

We headed back downstairs. Ashley was helping Jean Luc clear the table, their movements synchronized and comfortable. Everyone else had either gone to bed or were elsewhere, having their own panic attacks.

I sank back into my chair, suddenly aware of how bone-deep tired I was. My tailbone still throbbed from hitting the pavement the previous day. Suddenly that seemed like a really long time ago.

"Is your friend okay?" Ashley asked, appearing at my elbow with a cup of tea I hadn't asked for but desperately needed.

"She will be. Thank you."

"Of course." She hesitated, then sat in the chair beside me. "She said she was in Nice? That there were riots?"

I wrapped my hands around the warm cup, letting the heat seep into my skin as I shook my head slowly. "I don't know. She needs to rest now, but hopefully she can tell us more tomorrow."

Jean Luc emerged from the kitchen carrying a bottle of something amber and potent-looking. "Brandy," he announced. "For the nerves."

"You're a saint," I told him, holding out my teacup as he doctored it.

He poured generous measures into everyone's cups. When he got to Ashley, she accepted hers with a smile that made his ears turn pink.

Henry waved him off, his gaze still searching the shadows beyond the candlelight.

"You should drink that," I told him. "Doctor's orders."

"You're not a doctor."

"Details, as our wise hostess would say," I dismissed with a wave of my hand. "Drink."

His mouth twitched. Not quite a smile, but he let Jean Luc adulterate his coffee and took a sip.

I mirrored his action and the spicy tea burned its way down my throat and settled warmly in my stomach. The big white cat appeared from the shadows and jumped into my lap with zero warning and approximately three hundred pounds of force. I grunted, nearly spilling my drink.

"Hello to you, too."

He purred like a motorboat and began kneading my thighs with enthusiasm. I set down my glass and scratched behind his ears, feeling the tension in my shoulders ease fractionally.

13

Tuesday Morning

The old fashioned alarm clock on my bedside table was a doorstop. The screen was blank and no little red numbers announced the time.

The power was still out.

"Fantastic," I muttered, throwing back the covers.

Judging by the feeble light creeping in through the balcony doors, it was early, but there was no point in trying to go back to sleep. I showered in the dusky light, thankful that we still had hot water. There would be no blowdrying my hair, so I just scrubbed at it thoroughly with the towel and called it a day. Dressed in a pair of pleated slacks and a plain turtleneck, I pressed my ear to Darla's door, listening for any signs of movement.

Nothing.

That was probably for the best. As much as my curiosity ate at me, she needed the rest.

The stairs creaked under my feet as I descended. The light that filtered through the windows was brighter now, painting everything in shades of gold and making the dust motes dance like tiny fairies.

Voices drew me to the kitchen. Begonia stood at the stove, today's caftan a riot of oranges and yellows that hurt to look at before caffeine. Rose sat at the small table peeling potatoes, her white hair catching the light like a halo.

"Helena!" Begonia turned, brandishing a wooden spoon. "You are awake! Come, sit. I have coffee."

"You're my favorite person," I told her, collapsing into the chair across from Rose.

"I am everyone's favorite person," Begonia said cheerfully, setting a steaming mug in front of me. "Behold, the power of caffeine."

The coffee was strong and dark and exactly what I needed. I wrapped both hands around the mug and inhaled deeply, letting the warmth seep into my bones.

"Still no power?" I asked, though the answer was obvious.

"*Non.*" Begonia returned to the stove where she was doing something with eggs that smelled divine. "Jean Luc will drive into town this morning and check in with our local *gendarmes* and tell them about your friend's accident. He will bring back all of the news and gossip."

"I just checked on Darla and she's still sleeping." I took another sip of coffee. "I didn't want to wake her."

"Good. She needs rest." Begonia cracked another egg into the pan with unnecessary force. "What she described is very concerning."

"Indeed," I agreed.

Rose's hands never stilled as she worked on a potato. "I have lived too long," she said firmly, her tone almost angry. "I have lived through war. I have lived through occupation, through famine, through more stupidity than one person should have to witness." She set down the potato and glanced up at Begonia. "I have lived through the loss of my husband, and my son."

The kitchen went very quiet. Begonia crossed to the table and slid into the chair beside Rose, covering her hand.

"And now," Rose continued, "I have lived to see the end of the world."

"Rose," Begonia said softly, her usual effervescence dimmed. "Don't be dramatic. You can't say such things."

"Why not? Because it is frightening?" Rose picked up her potato again, her hands steady. "I am too old to be frightened. And too old to lie to myself."

"This isn't the end of the world," I said firmly. "I'm sure there's a reasonable explanation for everything."

Rose made a sound that might have been a laugh or a scoff. "You are a terrible liar, Helena Barrett. And my daughter-in-law is a terrible cook. You are burning the eggs, Begonia."

Begonia leapt up, cursing fluently in French. But the eggs she set in front of me a moment later were perfectly scrambled. She sat back down with her own plate, and pointed at me with her fork. "We will have a party tonight," she announced, her voice determinedly cheerful.

"A party?" I asked dubiously before popping a bit of egg into my mouth.

"Yes! If the power does not come back, the food in the refrigerator will spoil. So we will cook it all and have a feast. We will drink wine and tell stories by candlelight and refuse to let the end of the world—" She shot Rose a look. "—or whatever this is, steal our joy."

Grace appeared in the doorway. She looked like she hadn't slept at all—her hair was pulled back in a messy ponytail, her eyes red-rimmed, and she was clutching her phone like it was a life raft.

"Still nothing," she announced, her voice tight. "No signal, no internet, nothing. And my battery is about to die."

"Did you try turning it off and on again?" I asked.

Grace's look could have curdled milk. "Yes, Helena. I tried turning it off and on again. I also tried airplane mode, I tried removing the SIM card, I tried standing on one foot and sacrificing a chicken to the cell tower gods."

"Sarcasm is a good look on you," I said mildly.

"I learned from the best." She slumped into the chair beside me. "Begonia, does the inn have a landline?"

"Oui, but it is out as well," Begonia replied apologetically.

Grace turned her gaze back to me. "You don't have any reception either?"

I took a very long, very slow sip of my coffee.

"Helena?" Grace's voice was confused. "Is your phone dead too?"

"I haven't actually checked my phone," I admitted quietly, my gaze on the brown liquid swirling in my mug.

"You haven't checked it yet this morning?" Grace asked slowly.

"I haven't checked it since we left Paris."

The silence that followed could have stripped paint.

"You never—" Grace's voice climbed an octave. "Helena, it's been days. What do you mean you didn't check your phone?"

"I mean I haven't turned it on since we left Paris," I explained. "I'm on vacation. The whole point was to unplug."

"Unplug doesn't mean throw your phone into a volcano!"

"It's in my suitcase," I said defensively.

"Oh, well, as long as it's in your suitcase." Grace's hands were shaking now, though whether from anger or panic I couldn't tell. "Helena, there could be important messages."

Begonia had been watching this exchange with interest. "Grace, *chérie*, would you like some eggs?"

"No, thank you." Grace's fingers were white-knuckled around her phone. "I need to—I should—"

She stood abruptly and fled back toward the lobby.

"That went well," I muttered.

"You are being stubborn," Rose observed.

"It's one of my best qualities."

"It is one of your only qualities, from what I can see."

Begonia laughed, the sound warm and rich. "Rose, be nice to our guest."

"I am being nice. If I was not being nice, I would tell her that her hair looks like a bird tried to build a nest in it and gave up halfway through."

I touched my damp hair self-consciously.

"And on that note," I said, standing, "I'm going for a walk."

Outside, the morning air was crisp and clean, carrying the scent of lavender and rosemary. I settled on the front steps, the stone cool through my slacks. It was October already, and even here there were signs of fall. The big white cat appeared from nowhere and planted himself beside me, his bulk radiating warmth.

"So you've decided you like me now?" I asked him, running a hand down his wide back.

He purred in agreement.

I scratched him behind his ear and he sank his teeth into my hand just enough to hurt but not break the skin.

"Wow," I told him. "You're really giving mixed messages."

I leaned back and movement caught my eye. The herd of tiny goats rounded the corner of the house, their little legs churning as they trotted along. They flowed over every obstacle in their path, hopping onto benches and over tree stumps. As they approached the house, they cascaded over the stairs.

The smallest bounced off my legs, landing on its rump before jumping back up again.

"Hey," I barked. Not the first time I'd been mistaken for a tree, but still mildly offensive.

The goats closest to me went rigid. Their legs locked, they toppled sideways, and rolled across the gravel like furry bowling pins.

"Oh, for Christ's sake," I muttered, ignoring a twinge of guilt.

The ones who had fallen popped back up onto their feet and continued their journey toward the gate as if nothing had happened.

"You're ridiculous," I called after them.

The cat chirped in agreement.

I was shaking my head when I noticed a figure in the distance, walking along the road that led to the village.

"Hello!" I called out, standing. Here was an opportunity to find out what was going on, but the person didn't acknowledge me, just kept walking. *Bonjour Monsieur.*

The figure's head turned toward the sound of my voice and they changed direction, heading toward the inn.

"*Avez-vous* electricity?" I fumbled my pronunciation, my hand moving to shade my eyes against the sun.

It was a middle-aged man, wearing a brown suit. He was closer and moving faster now, revealing a pronounced limp.

"Are you hurt?" I called, my stomach twisting.

He began to flat out run, despite one leg nearly dragging behind him. I stumbled backward up the steps. "Stop," I said, my voice echoing through the silence of the morning.

The man didn't stop. He moved faster, passing the pillars standing at the entrance to the inn's courtyard. He rocketed across the gravel, heading straight toward me.

His eyes were sunken and red in his pale face, his mouth open in a silent scream.

I turned to run and careened straight into Henry's chest. He wrapped one arm around me as the crack of a gunshot split the morning air.

The world froze for a long moment.

My ears were ringing, but I lifted my head from Henry's shoulder and gathered my dignity as best I could. Henry's service weapon was in his hand and I braced myself as I turned back to the courtyard.

A figure was crumpled on the ground, motionless.

I took a step forward and Henry pulled me back.

"Inside," he said, his voice flat and professional. "Now."

My legs wouldn't move. I stood there, frozen, my gaze locked on the body sprawled in the gravel. I searched for movement desperately, but was also terrified of the possibility.

"Helena." Henry's hand closed around my arm, firm but not painful. "Go back inside."

This time my legs obeyed. I let him pull me through the doorway, into the cool dimness of the lobby. Behind us, the cat yowled once and darted away.

Begonia and Jean Luc burst from the kitchen, Rose close behind them.

"What was that noise?" Begonia's eyes were wide.

Henry released my arm and moved to the window, peering out carefully. "Everyone stay inside."

"Why?" Jean Luc asked. "What—"

"Just do it," Henry snapped.

He disappeared, the front door slamming as Grace came running down the stairs.

Her hand was warm as it wrapped around mine. "Helena," she whispered urgently. "What's going on? Was that...?" Her voice trailed off.

I nodded. "It all happened so quickly," I murmured flatly. "He wouldn't stop." A breath shuddered from my chest. "He—Henry—"

"He's dead," Henry said bluntly, reappearing in front of me. "I couldn't find any ID, but his skin was hot to the touch. I think he had this flu that's been going around." He scanned the lobby, taking in the shocked expressions. Jean Luc was standing beside Begonia, who clutched at his arm, her other hand pressed over her mouth.

"The flu?" Grace asked incredulously. "I thought I heard a gunshot."

"You did," Henry confirmed shortly. He turned to Begonia. "I'm so sorry for this disruption, *madame*." His demeanor was stiff and formal. "I'm going to need one of you to drive me into the village to report this to the authorities."

"I will get my keys," Jean Luc responded.

There were hurried footsteps that faded away, but my gaze was locked on Henry's face, tracing the vertical lines between his brows and the tightness at the outer corners of his eyes.

"Helena." He said my name as if it wasn't the first time. "Helena, I need you to focus."

I shook my head, blinking. "What?"

Henry had both of my hands in his now, his skin dry and warm. "I may not be coming back, Helena," he was saying.

"What?" I repeated, louder this time.

He sighed, starting over. "I have to report this incident to the local authorities and it seems likely that I will be taken into custody."

"No." I shook my head. "What are you talking about?"

"This is a major diplomatic incident. There's going to be an investigation." Henry squeezed my hands, his gaze intense. "I need you to stay here."

He shifted his attention away from me and my gaze fell to where his hands covered mine. His skin was darker than mine, covered in faint sunspots and fine dark hairs. "You should wear sunscreen," I murmured.

"Grace, stay with her," he was saying.

A soft hand landed on my shoulder and Begonia said, "We will all stay with her."

14

Tuesday Midmorning

Ashley

There was a dead body in the middle of the parking area. Ashley tore her gaze away, but her brain kept trying to process the shapes under Begonia's pretty flowered sheet.

It was just a lumpy pile, abandoned on the gravel.

If Henry, Mrs. Barrett's bodyguard, hadn't told them what it was, she never would have guessed "dead body" in a million years. Even after hearing the gunshot.

There had been no doubt what *that* was. She and Robert had rushed downstairs to find everyone standing in a hushed circle in the lobby, trying to decide what to do. When he found out that Jean Luc was driving into the village to report the incident to the local police, Robert had insisted that the two of them needed to go as well.

So here she was, holding tightly to Robert's hand and trying hard not to look at a dead body as she followed the handsome young Frenchman to his teeny tiny car.

"Shotgun," Robert announced, dropping Ashley's hand and sprinting to the passenger side of the little green Fiat.

Ashley frowned, but didn't argue, her thoughts still focused on the body behind them. She slipped quietly into the backseat of the car, not meeting Henry's gaze as the older man entered from the other side.

"Sorry," he murmured, wedging his knees toward the center behind Robert's seat.

Ashley forced a smile, but kept her head down. "It's okay," she said softly.

Jean Luc started the engine and the tiny car roared to life like a locomotive, vibrating wildly.

"Will this thing make it to town?" Robert asked skeptically.

"*Oui, Monsieur,*" he assured him, his voice calm and confident. "She may not be a young girl anymore, but this car is well-maintained and reliable."

Robert harrumphed in response and turned his head to the window.

Jean Luc caught her gaze in his rear view mirror, his eyes crinkling at the corners. "It is perfectly safe."

She smiled back as he put the car into gear, but her face fell as he carefully pulled around the draped form.

Everyone breathed a collective sigh of relief as the little car chugged through the gates and onto the road.

After a few minutes of silence broken only by the Fiat's laboring engine, Jean Luc caught her gaze again in the rearview mirror. "So," he began, "Is this your first trip to France?"

"It is," she answered, surprised. "I've always wanted to visit."

"And what do you think?" There was no mockery in his voice, just genuine curiosity.

"Well, we've been a little—" She caught herself, glancing at the back of Robert's head, "—stressed."

Beside her, Henry's mouth twitched. "That's one word for it."

Jean Luc nodded toward the road as they approached a curve. "The village is just ahead."

Ashley looked out the window, watching the country-side roll past. The golden fields seemed to run right up to the distant mountains and the sky was a perfect cloudless blue.

"Have you worked for Helena long?" she asked Henry, desperate to fill the silence.

"Long enough to know she's terrible at following orders."

"I can imagine." Ashley smiled, thinking about the way Helena had shut Robert down. She wished she could do that sometimes.

"Ashley's terrible at following orders too," Robert interjected. "She booked us at a bed and breakfast in the middle of nowhere instead of a proper hotel in the city."

The back of Ashley's neck heated. "You said you wanted something different. Something romantic."

"I wanted Paris. Wine and cheese and the Eiffel Tower. Not peeing by the side of the road and living off the grid in a drafty old house in the middle of nowhere."

Henry shifted beside her, and Ashley could feel the tension radiating from him. When he spoke, his voice was carefully neutral. "The inn is lovely. Begonia's very welcoming."

"Begonia is a mess," Robert muttered. "Did you see what she was wearing? She looks like a sideshow fortune teller."

Jean Luc's hands tightened on the steering wheel, his knuckles going white.

Ashley felt something crack inside her chest. "Robert, don't be rude."

Robert twisted in his seat to look at her, his eyebrows raised. "Excuse me?"

"Begonia is a wonderful hostess and has been nothing but kind to us. She gave us a room at three in the morning when she didn't have to. She's been—"

"She's been what, Ashley? *Nice*?" Robert's voice dripped with condescension. "She's in the hospitality industry. Being nice is literally her job."

The car slowed as they approached the village. There were stone buildings ahead, narrow streets, and the church steeple rising above it all.

And a small silver sedan embedded in the side of a building.

"Oh my god," she breathed.

The car's front end was crumpled and the building's wall had partially collapsed, stones and mortar scattered across the street. The car's doors hung open, and the windshield was shattered.

Jean Luc brought the Fiat to a stop, his face pale. "That is Madame Chevalier's home," he said quietly.

They sat there for a moment, staring at the wreckage. No one moved. No one spoke.

Finally, Henry opened his door. "We're not going to be able to drive around that. So it looks like we're walking from here."

They climbed out of the car, Ashley's legs shaky as she stood. The street was eerily quiet. No people. No sounds of daily life. Just the wind rustling through abandoned flower boxes and the distant caw of a crow.

"The police station is this way," Jean Luc said, gesturing down a narrow alley between two stone buildings. "It is not far."

They followed him single file, their footsteps echoing off the ancient cobblestones. Ashley's heart hammered against her ribs and her imagination went into overdrive. Every shadow loomed threateningly. Every doorway hid something terrible.

The buildings they passed were either damaged or shuttered tight. A tiny grocery store with its windows smashed, boxes and cans scattered across the floor inside. A café with overturned tables and broken glass glittering on the tile. A bakery with its door hanging off the hinges.

"Where is everyone?" Ashley whispered.

"Social distancing," Henry said. He'd positioned himself at the rear of their small group, constantly looking back over his shoulder. "Maybe."

The police station was a squat brick building on the town square, with blue shutters and a French flag hanging limp in the still air. The door was closed but not locked. Jean Luc pushed it open slowly, the hinges creaking.

"*Bonjour*," he called out. "*Il y a quelqu'un?*"

Silence.

They stepped inside. The tiny reception area was empty, papers scattered across the front desk, a coffee cup overturned and a brown stain spread across a stack of reports.

Henry and Jean Luc shared a meaningful look and turned away without a word.

They emerged back into the sunlight and Ashley squinted against the brightness. In the center of the town square a fountain burbled merrily, and pieces of what might have been tables and awnings were scattered across the cobblestones like kindling.

Robert cleared his throat. "I think we should go back to the inn now."

For once, Ashley had to agree with him, but Jean Luc was shaking his head.

He started off in the wrong direction and Ashley rushed after him, grabbing at his hand. "Where are you going?"

"I must check on my friends," he said urgently, his steps picking up.

Henry appeared on Jean Luc's other side. "Where do your friends live?"

"There." Jean Luc pointed to a building on the far side of the square. "Gaspard and his wife live above the *poissonnerie*."

They crossed the square in silence, their footsteps echoing off the stone buildings. The little shop had a sign with a large fish and a red door that was closed tight, its window dark. Jean Luc knocked, the sound unnaturally loud in the stillness.

Nothing.

He knocked again, harder. "Gaspard? *C'est Jean Luc.* Are you there?"

A crash from inside made them all step back. Then angry shouting in rapid French. The door remained closed.

"Gaspard!" Jean Luc called. "*Avez-vous besoin d'aide?*"

More shouting. Something heavy hit the door from inside, making it shudder in its frame. The voice was hoarse, raw, almost unrecognizable as human.

"We should go," Ashley said quietly.

"But—"

Henry placed a hand on the other man's shoulder. "Now, Jean Luc."

They backed away from the shop. Behind them, Robert had gone pale, his earlier bravado evaporating.

"What the fuck is wrong with everyone?" Robert whispered.

Jean Luc was staring at the door, his face stricken. "I have known Gaspard my whole life."

Ashley placed a gentle hand on his arm. "I'm so sorry."

"Where else?" Henry interrupted gently. "Who else do you need to check on?"

Jean Luc swallowed hard. "Bertrand. He lives two streets over." His voice cracked. "He is a family friend."

They found the house easily—a narrow stone building with yellow shutters and flower boxes that had gone dry. Jean Luc knocked, his knuckles white against the dark wood.

"Bertrand? It is Jean Luc. I am here to check on you."

Silence. Then footsteps inside, slow and shuffling.

"Jean Luc?" The voice was muffled through the door but recognizably human. Strained but coherent.

"Yes! Are you okay? What is happening?"

"Go home." Bertrand's voice was firm despite the tremor underneath. "Go back to the inn and lock the doors. Don't let anyone in. Do you understand?"

"But—"

"Everyone is sick. Angry sick." A pause. "Crazy sick." His voice broke. "Please, Jean Luc, go home. I am sorry."

"Bertrand—"

"Go!"

Something crashed inside the house. Jean Luc stumbled backward, his face ashen.

Henry grabbed his arm. "Come on. We need to leave."

They were halfway across the square when Robert stopped dead, staring at something beyond the fountain.

"Holy shit," he breathed softly

Ashley followed his gaze and her stomach dropped.

Three people were standing in one of the side streets. Two men and a woman, all middle-aged, all dressed in ordinary clothes that were now torn and stained. They swayed in place like they were drunk, their movements jerky and uncoordinated.

Ashley stumbled to a stop, her shoe brushing against a discarded can at the edge of the street and sending it rolling a few feet. The clatter of the metal against the cobblestones echoed through the square.

The change in the three villagers was instantaneous. The swaying stopped. Their heads snapped around in perfect unison, fixing on Ashley and the others with an intensity that made her skin crawl.

"Back away slowly," Henry said quietly. "Don't make any sudden movements."

"Fuck that," Robert breathed, then he turned and ran.

The three figures took a step forward. Then another.

"Run!" Henry barked.

Ashley had done a 5K in college and hadn't embarrassed herself. But sprinting through a medieval French village while being chased by crazy people? That was a completely different experience.

Her lungs burned. Her feet ached with every impact against the unforgiving stone. And behind her, those people were making sounds that would haunt her nightmares forever. They weren't screaming, they were keening. It was a high-pitched, raspy sound that echoed off the buildings.

And the icing on the cake was the sight of her fiancé running at least twenty yards ahead of her, his dress shoes slapping against the cobblestones. He hadn't looked back once.

Ex-fiancé.

Henry and Jean Luc ran on either side of her. Jean Luc was tall and lean and no doubt could have outpaced them both in a heartbeat, but instead he stuck right by her side.

Up ahead Robert darted to the left. The three of them followed, Ashley veering around the corner so sharply she nearly lost her footing.

Henry steaded her with a hand under her elbow and Jean Luc's arm braced against her back, the two men herding her down a narrow alley. Laundry hung overhead on lines strung between buildings, white sheets swaying above them.

Ashley glanced over her shoulder, her breath coming in ragged gasps. Behind them, their pursuers rounded the corner. There were more than three now. Maybe six? Eight?

"There!" Henry pointed ahead where Robert was ducking into a small shop with green shutters and a door that was, miraculously, hanging slightly open.

Robert disappeared inside and Henry sprinted ahead. The door began to swing closed and Henry leapt forward, kicking it back open and moving forward aggressively. Ashley stumbled through after him, followed by Jean Luc. Henry slammed the door shut behind them and immediately started looking for something to barricade it with.

Ashley stood panting in the middle of the shop. It was some kind of antique store. Dust motes danced in the thin light filtering through the shutters. Shelves lined the walls, crammed with books, china figurines, tarnished silver, and a random assortment of tchotchkes.

"It smells like my grandmother's house," she noted blankly.

"Help me," Henry grunted, shoving against a massive wooden armoire.

Ashley lurched forward and Jean Luc leaned in beside her. Together the three of them wrestled the piece of furniture in front of the door just as something heavy slammed into it from outside.

Ashley jumped, a squeak escaping her throat. Robert was standing across the room, peering through a gap in the shutters.

"There's got to be a dozen of them out there," he said, his voice tight.

Another body hit the door and the armoire shuddered.

"How long will that hold?" Ashley asked, hating how small her voice sounded.

"Long enough." Henry was already moving, checking the other rooms. "Let's find another exit."

"This way." Jean Luc led them through to the back of the shop, past a small kitchen area. The back door was solid wood with a brass lever handle.

Henry tried it. It didn't budge.

"There's a window," Jean Luc said, pointing to a narrow opening above the counter.

From the front of the shop came the sound of breaking glass. More impacts against the door, rhythmic now. Determined.

"They're going to get in," Robert said. His face had gone gray, his earlier panic crystallizing into something harder. "We're trapped."

"Don't panic." Henry's voice was calm, which somehow made everything worse. "We just need to—"

"I'll go," Jean Luc interrupted.

Everyone turned to look at him.

"The window leads to the alley behind. I will go out, make noise, lead them away. Wait ten seconds and then go out the front."

"Absolutely not," Ashley said immediately.

Jean Luc smiled at her, quick and sweet despite the circumstances. "It is okay. I know these streets. I can lose them and circle back. I will meet you at the car."

"Jean Luc—" Henry started.

"There is no time." He was already climbing onto the counter, his movements quick and efficient. "Count to ten after you hear me shout, then go."

More crashing from the front room. The sound of the armoire grinding against the floor.

Jean Luc pushed open the window and hauled himself through with surprising athleticism. For a moment his legs dangled, then he was gone.

Ashley's heart was trying to slam its way out of her chest. She pressed her hand against her sternum, the rapid thump-thump-thump beating her palm.

"He's going to run," Robert said. "There's no way—"

"Hey!" Jean Luc's voice rang out from the front of the building, loud and clear. "Hey! *Regardez-moi, bande d'idiots!*"

The banging on the front door stopped abruptly. Ashley held her breath, counting in her head.

One Mississippi. Two Mississippi.

Footsteps faded. The keening grew fainter.

Five Mississippi. Six Mississippi.

They moved back through to the front room. The door was hanging crooked in its frame, the armoire shoved several inches from where they'd left it. But the street beyond was empty.

Eight Mississippi. Nine Mississippi.

Henry eased the door open, checking both directions. "Let's go."

Robert pushed past him, bursting through the door like he'd been shot from a cannon. Henry pulled Ashley through the door and then they were running.

Ashley's side had developed a sharp stitch that felt like someone was stabbing her with a hot poker. Her lungs burned. Her vision had narrowed to a tunnel focused on

Robert's back ahead of her and the uneven cobblestones beneath her feet.

They ran past the church with its silent bell tower. Past a café with chairs scattered across its terrace. Past a pharmacy with a green cross sign hanging crooked above the door. The village blurred around them.

Robert was pulling ahead again. The gap between them widening with every step.

When they saw the tiny Fiat still sitting in the middle of the road, Ashley wanted to sag with relief, but she kept running.

Robert skidded to a halt beside the car, tearing open the driver side door and throwing himself into the seat. He clutched at the steering wheel, flipping down the sun visor.

"He took the keys," Robert yelled, frantically searching through the center console.

Ignoring him, Ashley turned back toward the village, searching the road behind them.

"Where is he?" Her voice came out high and strained. "Do you think he made it?"

"He'll catch up," Henry said, but he was watching the road too, his expression tight.

"We should go back." Ashley took a step toward the village.

Henry's hand on her shoulder stopped her. "He knows this area. He'll find another way out."

"He's probably dead," Robert said flatly. He'd exited the car and moved to stand beside them.

"Shut up, Robert." The words came out before Ashley could stop them.

He turned to stare at her, genuine surprise on his face. "Excuse me?"

"I said *shut up*." She was shaking now, adrenaline and fear and anger making her voice stronger than she felt. "He saved us. The least you can do is not—"

A crash in the bushes to their left made them all jump.

Jean Luc burst through the hedge, leaves in his hair and his shirt torn at the shoulder. He was breathing hard but grinning.

"*Bonjour*," he said cheerfully.

Ashley didn't think. She just moved, closing the distance between them and throwing her arms around his neck hard enough to make him stagger.

"You made it," she said into his shoulder.

"*Oui.*" His arms came up to steady her, his hands warm against her back. "I told you I would."

She pulled back just enough to look at him, her hands still gripping his shoulders. "That was the stupidest thing I've ever seen anyone do."

His grin widened. "Like an American action movie, no?"

Ashley's laugh had an edge of hysteria. "Totally," she agreed.

"This reunion is truly touching," Robert's voice was sharp. "But can we get the hell out of here now?"

15
Tuesday Midday

Helena

I stood at the window, watching the empty road, my hands gripping the sill hard enough to make my knuckles white.

"They'll be fine," Begonia said from beside me, though her voice lacked conviction.

"Of course they will." I released the windowsill and flexed my fingers, willing blood back into them.

Darla appeared on the stairs, moving slowly. She'd changed into what had to be more of Begonia's clothes—a flowing skirt and soft sweater that made her look like she belonged in a pastoral painting. William dashed past her, careening down the stairs and directly toward a display of delicate porcelain figurines.

Begonia intercepted him.

"*Mon petit*, it is so lovely to see you feeling better this morning, but perhaps we should—"

"I'm going to touch every single thing in this room," William announced with the confidence of a tiny dictator.

William reached for a porcelain shepherdess with an expression of pure menace.

Begonia conjured a wooden bowl of walnuts from thin air and presented it as a sacrificial offering.

"These are much more interesting, yes? You can crack them."

William studied the walnuts with suspicion. "How?"

"With your teeth."

His eyes lit up and I suppressed a shudder at the dental emergency waiting to happen.

Darla, moving much more slowly, came to stand at my side. The bruising on her face had darkened overnight to shades of purple and yellow that made me wince in sympathy.

"How are you feeling?" I asked.

"Like I got hit by a truck." She managed a weak smile. "Which is basically what happened."

William abandoned the walnuts and launched himself at his mother. She caught him with practiced ease despite her obvious pain, one hand cradling the back of his head.

"Mommy, I'm cracking nuts with my teeth!"

"That's wonderful, honey."

Rose materialized in the kitchen doorway. "Everyone come and sit," she commanded. "We drink tea. We pretend to be civilized."

"I don't want tea," William announced.

"Good. Tea is not for babies." Rose set a tray of cups out on the table with a decisive clink as I settled into a chair beside Grace.

William's face scrunched up in outrage. "I'm not a baby! I want tea!"

"Too late. You had your chance."

I bit back a laugh as the ornery old woman poured tea into delicate cups with surprisingly steady hands. She passed me a cup and I wrapped my hands around it, grateful for the warmth and the familiar ritual of it all. We were drinking tea while the world apparently went to shit outside. How very British of us.

"So," Grace said, cradling her own cup. "Should we talk about the dead body in the driveway?"

"Must we?" I took a sip of tea. It was strong and milky.

"There's a dead body, Mommy?" William's head popped up from where he'd been examining the rejected walnuts.

Darla's face went pale. "William, honey, why don't you—"

"Did you see it? Was there blood? How did the body die?" The questions tumbled out with alarming enthusiasm.

"William James Blackstone," Darla's voice took on the universal maternal tone that had its own gravitational pull. "That's enough."

William deflated slightly but his eyes were still bright with morbid curiosity.

"The goats faint," I said into the silence.

Everyone turned to look at me.

"I'm sorry, what?" Darla blinked.

"The goats. They faint when they get startled. It's the most ridiculous thing I've ever seen." I looked at William. "Would you like to go see them?"

His face transformed, the dead body temporarily forgotten. "Fainting goats? Really?"

"Really. They just lock up and fall over. It's hilarious."

"Can I make them faint?"

"Oh, definitely."

Darla looked torn between gratitude and concern. "I don't know if—"

"Grace, will you show William the goats while I talk to Darla?" I turned to my assistant with my most winning smile.

Grace's expression suggested she was reconsidering her life choices. With a sigh she set her cup of tea on the table and pushed to her feet. "Sure. Why not?"

William was already bouncing around the room with renewed energy. "Let's go! I'm going to make them all faint!"

"Please don't traumatize the livestock," Begonia called after them weakly as Grace led him toward the back door.

The door closed behind them and I let out a long breath.

"You are just a little bit evil," Begonia observed.

"Yes." I set down my teacup. "We need to know exactly what happened in Nice."

Rose made a sound of approval. "Finally. Someone with sense."

Darla nodded slowly. "I'll tell you what I can."

"If you're up to talking about it."

She looked down, her hands wrapped around her teacup. "Where do you want me to start?"

"You said there were riots? Were they violent?"

Darla was quiet for a moment, staring into her tea like it might hold the answers. When she spoke, her voice was soft but steady.

"Beyond violent. The news called it *la démence*. People were running a fever and going crazy, attacking each other, destroying property, setting fires. The city shut down completely. Dan said we needed to get out of the populated area, so we got in the car and just drove."

Begonia had gone very still. "What about the local authorities?"

"We saw police. They were overwhelmed. Some of them were—" Darla's voice broke. "Some of them were infected too. Attacking people they were supposed to be protecting."

My stomach twisted. "What was the news saying about the infection? Were they still calling it a flu or a prion virus?"

"I don't know. Maybe? Dan said it was like nothing he'd ever seen. He was Special Forces. He's seen combat, dealt with riots, terrorist attacks—" She stopped, swallowing hard. "He said this was worse."

"What happened to Dan?" I asked gently.

Darla shook her head, fresh tears tracking down her cheeks. "He seemed fine. Professional. In control. Then he started complaining about being hot. We had the air conditioning on full blast and he was still sweating through his shirt. His eyes were bloodshot." She looked up at me. "Then the van hit us and everything went crazy."

Rose refilled Darla's teacup without asking. "Drink," she commanded. "It helps."

"Does it?" Darla's laugh was bitter. "They survived the crash," she stated bluntly. "Dan pulled Jacob from the car and..." Darla's voice faltered.

The silence that followed was heavy.

"The man this morning," I said carefully. "The one Henry shot. He was showing the same symptoms."

William came crashing back into the kitchen, Grace hot on his heels.

"Stranger danger! Stranger danger!" The little boy was yelling.

We all jumped. My teacup hit the table with a crash, hot liquid splashing across the surface.

"William!" Darla was on her feet, sweeping the boy into her arms.

"There's a man in the garden," Grace gasped.

We all rushed to the windows.

I got there first, my heart hammering against my ribs.

The garden was chaos.

The goats were in full panic mode, their tiny bodies rigid as they toppled over and popped back up only to faint again. A man was running around, chasing them, in what had once been a business suit, his white shirt now filthy and torn. His movements were jerky, uncoordinated, and his face—

"Jesus Christ," I breathed.

He had red eyes, just like the man this morning. But this one wasn't coming at me, he was lurching after the tiny goats with single-minded determination.

The smallest goat ran into the bench and collapsed, legs straight out from its little body as if it had been electrocuted. The man reached down.

Somewhere behind me, William was screaming, but I was already turning toward the door. The kitchen was a blur of copper pots and hanging herbs. Begonia's large cast iron skillet sat on top of the cooktop. My hands closed around the handle as I passed the stove. It was heavy, reassuringly solid, probably older than I was.

It was perfect.

"Helena, what are you—"

I didn't stop to answer Grace's question. I ran out the door and toward the man who now had the little goat in his arms and was raising it toward his face.

"Hey!" I shouted. "Hey, asshole! Over here!"

The man's head snapped toward me with unnatural speed.

"That's right, you piece of shit. Come and get me."

He dropped the tiny goat, who bounced onto the ground, stiff as a board. Then he turned his red eyes toward me.

"Well," I said. "Shit."

He lunged.

I swung the skillet with everything I had. It connected with his shoulder with a meaty thunk that rattled up my arms. He stumbled but didn't go down.

Begonia appeared beside me, wielding a big wood rolling pin like a baseball bat, catching him across the back. "You do not have a reservation, *monsieur!*"

He spun toward her, his hands grasping. I brought the skillet down on his arm and heard something crack.

"His head!" Begonia shouted. "Aim for his head!"

"I'm trying!" I swung again, catching him a glancing blow across the temple. Blood welled up, shockingly red against his pale skin.

He didn't even seem to notice.

His hands closed around my wrist and I felt his nails dig into my skin. His breath was hot and foul, his face twisted into something barely human.

Begonia screamed something in French that I was pretty sure violated several obscenity laws and brought the rolling pin down on the back of his skull with a crack that made me wince.

He dropped to his knees, finally, but his hand was still locked around my wrist in a death grip.

I raised the skillet again, my arm shaking with adrenaline and exertion.

The gunshot was deafening.

The man's head snapped back and he crumpled, his hand finally releasing me as he slid to the ground.

I turned to see Rose standing in the doorway, an ancient hunting rifle braced against her tiny shoulder. The gun looked almost as big as she was.

"Amateurs," she said disdainfully, lowering the weapon. "I can tell you girls have never fought Nazis."

"Holy shit," I breathed.

"Holy shit," Begonia agreed.

16

Tuesday Afternoon

The sound of the Fiat's struggling engine was the most beautiful thing I'd heard all day. Granted, it was barely past one, but I was already on my second alcoholic beverage. I had been camped out on the front steps of the inn for nearly an hour, clutching a glass of wine and the cast iron frying pan. I wasn't sure which of them was holding me together at this point.

The little green car chugged through the gates and Henry lurched from the back seat before it even rolled to a stop, his face pale and tight.

"What happened? Is everything okay?" I said, the drape-covered dead body still between us.

"Define okay," he responded, taking in my odd assortment of accessories.

Ashley tumbled out of the back seat after him, her face flushed and her hair wild. Jean Luc brought the car to a complete stop and turned off the noisy engine. In the sudden silence he exited the driver's side, followed by Robert.

"There's another body in the garden," I announced without preamble.

The group froze mid-step.

Henry's eyes drifted back to the frying pan in my hand and I shrugged. "Rose shot him, but I got a few good licks in."

Ashley made a sound that might have been a laugh or a sob. "Oh, my god."

A chorus of bleating erupted from inside the house, high-pitched and insistent.

"Are those—" Jean Luc started.

"Goats," I confirmed.

"In the house?" Henry's expression was suspiciously flat.

There was more bleating from within, accompanied by the sound of something ceramic hitting the floor and shattering.

I handed my glass to Henry. "I can't wait to hear about *your* day."

He took the glass from my hand and drained it in one go.

Inside, goats perched on furniture, investigated corners, and generally treated the entire first floor of the inn as if it was designed specifically for their entertainment. The cat had retreated to the top of a bookshelf, where he hovered like a furious white cloud, his tail lashing.

William was in heaven. He'd discovered that if he clapped his hands, any goats near him would lock up and topple over. He was working his way from room to room systematically, testing his theory.

"William, honey, maybe give the goats a break," Darla suggested weakly from where she sat at the kitchen table.

"But Mommy, look! It's like a freeze ray!"

"Fascinating," Darla said without enthusiasm.

"The goats," Henry repeated slowly. "Are in the house."

"This is insane," Robert said, standing in the doorway to the kitchen. "This is absolutely fucking insane. We need to leave. Now. Get in the car and drive to—"

"Where?" Ashley's voice was sharp. "The village is over-run. The road is blocked anyway."

My eyebrows shot up. "Overrun? Blocked?" I turned to Henry, who just shook his head.

Ashley continued. "And even if we could get out to the highway, that's a mess too and Nice is a disaster zone." She swung her arms out wide. "Where exactly do you think we should go, Robert?"

"Somewhere. Anywhere that isn't here—"

"Miss Helena saved the goats from the zombie." William's gruff little voice cut across Robert's spiraling and every eye in the room turned to look at the little boy with various expressions of dismay.

"There is no such thing as zombies," I told him firmly. "That man was just very sick."

"You think this is the flu?" Henry asked, as if he already knew the answer.

I nodded. "It seems likely." I pinned him with a stare. "But what did Ashley mean by *overrun*? What did the police say?"

Henry sighed and pulled out a chair. He waved the others forward and soon everyone was seated around the table with varying expressions of trepidation.

"So," I said, looking around the table. "Who wants to start?"

"The village is fucked," Robert said bluntly. "That's the short version."

Ashley and Jean Luc visibly winced but no one contradicted him.

A muscle throbbed along Henry's jaw. "We encountered multiple individuals who were behaving in an erratic and aggressive manner. The police station was abandoned. Most of the buildings are either damaged or locked up tight and the road into the village is blocked by an abandoned vehicle embedded into the side of one of the houses." He shook his head. "There was no way to get the Fiat around it."

"We spoke to Bertrand. He was home but he would not open the door," Jean Luc said quietly. "He warned us to stay inside and lock the doors."

"How did he seem?" Rose asked.

"Frightened," Jean Luc said. "But not sick. He said everyone in the village is sick. Angry sick, he called it."

"That tracks with what Darla described," I said. "High fever, dementia, aggression."

"And trying to eat goats," Begonia added. "Do not forget that part."

"No," I assured her. "I'm not likely to forget that part."

"We saw them," Ashley's soft voice pierced the silence. "In the square. Their eyes were red and they were just, like, shaking or something. And when they saw us, they ran toward us, screaming."

"The kid is right," Robert said flatly.

We all just stared.

"I know how it sounds." He leaned forward, his eyes too wide. "But I've seen this movie. Hell, we've all seen this movie. This is how it starts. The infection, the rage, people turning into—"

"Please don't," I begged.

"Zombies!" Robert slapped his palm against the table hard enough to make his coffee cup rattle. "That little kid is smart enough to see it. We're in the middle of a goddamn zombie apocalypse!"

At the table beside me, Darla rose quickly, bundling William up and out of the kitchen without a backward glance. Grace pressed her hands over her mouth.

"They're not zombies," Henry said. His voice was calm, which somehow made Robert's hysteria more pronounced by contrast. "They're sick. Infected with something that's making them violent and irrational."

"That's literally what a zombie is!"

"Zombies are dead," I pointed out. "Or undead."

Robert laughed, high and sharp. "Oh, well, thanks for clearing that up, Madame First Lady. Let's quibble over semantics while they tear our flesh from our bones."

The room went very still.

"Robert." Ashley's voice was quiet but firm. "Stop."

"Stop? Stop?!" He turned on her, his face flushing. "We're all going to die here, Ashley. You picked a real winner."

"Enough." I stood, planting my hands on the table and leaning forward. "Robert, I understand you're frightened. We all are. But hysteria will get us nowhere."

He stared at me for a long moment, his mouth working like he was trying to find words caustic enough to match his anger. Then he shoved back from the table and grabbed Ashley's arm.

"We're leaving," he announced.

"Robert, let go—"

"We're getting in the car and we're driving to the coast. There has to be a boat, a ship, something. We're getting the hell out of France before this gets worse."

"From what Darla said," I pointed out. "It's worse in Nice."

"We'll take our chances!" Robert was already pulling Ashley toward the door.

"Robert, you're hurting me—"

"Let her go," Jean Luc said. He'd risen from his chair, his hands clenched at his sides.

Robert laughed. "Or what? You'll challenge me to a duel? This isn't your business, boy."

"She asked you to let go."

"She's my girlfriend. She'll do what I tell her."

"Ex-girlfriend," Ashley said. Her voice was shaking but clear. "We're done."

Robert's face went through several shades of red before settling on puce. "You ungrateful little—"

Henry moved. One moment he was standing by the window, the next he was between Robert and Ashley, his hand clamped around Robert's wrist.

"Let go," Henry said quietly. "Now."

For a second, I thought Robert might actually try to fight him. His whole body tensed, his free hand curling into a fist. Then whatever survival instinct he still possessed kicked in and he flung Ashley's arm away from him with a grunt of disgust.

"You're all in denial," he muttered, backing toward the door. "When this whole place gets overrun, don't come crying to me."

He stormed out, his footsteps thundering up the stairs.

In the silence that followed, Ashley sank back into her chair and pressed her hands to her face.

"I'm sorry," she whispered.

"You have nothing to apologize for," I told her firmly.

Begonia stood behind her chair and placed a gentle hand on Ashley's shoulder. "Men like that," she said softly, "they show you who they are when things get difficult. It is a gift, no? Now you know."

Ashley's laugh was shaky but genuine. "Some gift."

"Better to know now than later." Begonia sank back into her chair with a sigh.

"Thank you." Ashley gave Begonia a tired smile and then looked at Jean Luc, who was still standing rigid, his jaw tight. "And thank you. For what you did." She turned back to Begonia and explained, "He led them away so that we could escape."

His expression softened. "It was nothing."

"You saved us," she corrected firmly.

I cleared my throat. I hated to interrupt their moment, but we needed more information. "How many did you see? Infected people, I mean."

Henry was still standing, staring out the windows into the courtyard. "Maybe a dozen in the square. There are probably more in the buildings if people were barricading themselves in like Bertrand." He crossed his arms, his shoulders tight with tension. "We should assume we're on our own and plan accordingly. Hunker down. Wait it out."

"We are all agreed?" Begonia looked around the table. "Everyone will stay and we will make it through together?"

One by one, everyone nodded.

"Good," Rose said. "Now we need to deal with the bodies."

***

We were a sad little procession, weaving our way awkwardly through the garden in the fading light.

"This way," Rose directed, leading us around the edge of the back field with a flashlight, the old hunting rifle resting on her shoulder.

"How much further?" I gasped, adjusting my grip on the sheet.

"Not much. Do not be a baby."

Begonia and I shared a glance over our still burden but kept our mouths shut.

Behind us, Henry and Jean Luc struggled with the other body, their labored breathing punctuated with the occasional grunt.

"This well was decommissioned, right?" I clarified for the third time, desperate for distraction from the burning in my shoulders. "We aren't going to be contaminating the water table?"

Rose's laughter floated back to us. "Yes, yes, I am sure. These are not the first bodies that have found their final resting place here."

"What?" I stumbled to a stop, almost my losing my grip.

We'd reached the back of the property now, where the cultivated gardens gave way to wilder growth. Trees pressed close, their branches creating deep shadows in the gathering dusk.

"It is here," Rose said, pointing with the flashlight.

The old well sat in a clearing about two hundred yards from the main house, half-hidden by overgrown vegetation. The wooden cover was rotted through in places.

Rose set down her rifle and pushed the cover aside with surprising strength for someone so small. The well gaped open, a circle of darkness that seemed to swallow the dwindling light.

"How deep is it?" I asked.

"Deep enough," Rose said. She was staring into the well, her expression distant. "My grandfather dug it himself, you know. With his own hands. But he did not dig deep enough. The water was no good—too close to the surface, too much contamination from the limestone."

Henry and Jean Luc brought the first body forward. The sheet had come partially unwrapped, revealing the man's face. His eyes were still open, clouded and vacant.

I looked away as they pushed him over the edge. A thump sounded from below.

When Henry and Jean Luc stepped back, Begonia and I maneuvered the second man up and over. Another thump.

"Then the well dried up entirely. My father dug the new well closer to the house," Rose continued, it was fully dark now but her voice was calm. "Deeper. Better. The water was sweet and cold. This one, he left it. Too much work to fill in, he said. Why bother?"

She turned to look at us, her eyes glittering in the moonlight.

"Then the Germans came. Young men in their nice uniforms, thinking they owned France." Her voice was matter-of-fact, conversational. "My friends and I were just girls. Eighteen, nineteen. We had nothing. No weapons, no training. But we were pretty."

"Rose," Begonia breathed.

"We would lure them out here. To the old well. For privacy, we said." Rose's hands gripped the stone edge. "A quick twist of the knife and then we would push them in."

The silence was absolute.

"How many?" Henry asked quietly.

Rose shrugged. "I did not count. The well is very deep. It has held many secrets."

"Jesus Christ," I whispered.

"Jesus had nothing to do with it," Rose said sharply. "Just angry French girls and stupid German boys." She looked around at all of us, her expression challenging.

"I'm not judging," I said quickly. "I'm amazed."

"You should be. We were magnificent." She picked up a small stone and dropped it into the well. At the faint ping of its landing, she nodded approvingly.

Begonia had gone very quiet, staring at her mother-in-law with new eyes. "Did your father know? About the Germans?"

"Of course. Where do you think we got the knives?"

Jean Luc made a strangled sound, then coughed to clear his throat. "Should we say something?" he asked quietly.

"Like what?" I asked.

"A prayer? Some kind of words?"

Everyone was looking at me.

"They were someone's sons," I said finally. "Maybe someone's fathers or brothers or husbands. They were not monsters, they were sick. Whatever they became at the end, they were people first. So—" I paused, searching for words. "May they rest in peace. And may whatever caused this end soon."

"Amen," Begonia whispered.

"That was very nice," Rose said approvingly. "Much better than what I said for the Nazis."

"What did you say for the Nazis?" I asked.

"*Bon débarras*. Good riddance."

A surprised laugh burst from my chest. And once I started, I couldn't stop. Begonia joined in, then Jean Luc. Even Henry's mouth twitched.

We stood there in the gathering darkness, laughing like lunatics at the edge of a makeshift mass grave.

"Come," Rose said finally, turning back toward the house. "It is getting dark. We need wine."

"Yes, please," I agreed.

We followed the beam of Rose's flashlight as we trudged back across the field. The house appeared ahead of us, its windows glowing with candlelight, smoke rising from the chimney.

It looked like something from a postcard. Peaceful. Idyllic.

"It could be worse," Begonia said, linking her arm through mine.

"How?"

"We could be out there." She nodded toward the darkness beyond the property. "Instead of in here with friends and wine and cheese."

"And goats," I added.

Begonia nodded. "And goats."

"And a tiny rebel assassin."

"That too."

17
Wednesday

Robert never reappeared that night, but I assumed Begonia saw him when she helped Ashley move her things to another room. He was also missing the next morning when the rest of us gathered around the courtyard table for a late breakfast. The sun was already high in the sky, burning off the previous night's chill. The meal was simple—bread, cheese, eggs—but good. Unfortunately, my stomach was too knotted to properly appreciate it.

Darla was sitting beside William, looking more herself after a day of rest. Her bruises had deepened to spectacular shades of purple and yellow, but the hollow look in her eyes had receded slightly.

I started the conversation as gently as I could. "We need to gather as much information as we can. Darla, do you remember anything else about what happened?"

She glanced down at William, who seemed to be happily shoving buttered bread into his face. She was wearing another Begonia outfit, a colorful wrap over her shoulders. "Before we left Paris, Dan and Jacob were talking about the daily security briefing. They were concerned that there would be another lockdown."

Henry leaned forward. "That was on Saturday?" When she nodded he cut his eyes to me and we shared a long look. "We never got a briefing on Saturday," he confirmed, before shifting back to Darla. "Do you remember anything else from the briefing?"

Darla set down her spoon and closed her eyes, her brow furrowed. "So much has happened since then." Her voice was soft. "We were packing up everything at the hotel and Dan was talking to Jacob." Her eyes opened and she glanced toward me with tears in her eyes. "I was tuning them out."

"There's no way you could have known," I reassured her.

William was building a fortress out of bread crusts, seemingly unconcerned with the adult conversation happening around him. On his other side, Grace occasionally redirected his architectural ambitions away from his water glass.

"Maurice, the cyclist at the market," Begonia said quietly. "He had this flu. He crashed his bicycle deliberately. His eyes were red, streaming with tears. And he was so angry."

"Same with Dan," Darla added. "It helps, knowing it wasn't his fault—" her voice broke.

William looked up from his bread fortress, his small face worried. "Mama?"

Darla took a calming breath and ran a hand over his curls. "It's okay, baby. Mama's just tired."

"We'll be okay," Rose said firmly. Her small frame radiated a surprising amount of authority. "France has survived wars, famines, occupation. We will survive this too."

"We should inventory our supplies," I said. "Figure out rationing if it comes to that."

Henry leaned forward, catching Jean Luc's gaze. "And we should see what we can do to fortify the house and property."

Jean Luc nodded. "We should close the gate." He grimaced. "I should have thought of that yesterday."

Begonia patted his hand. "We're all doing our best, *mon cher*." She waved toward the open end of the courtyard. "We have the roll of fencing from the old chicken coop, do we not? Maybe we could close off the courtyard and put the goats out here."

We all turned to look at the french doors, where several small pointy faces were pressed against the glass.

"That would be good," I said.

As if sensing their imminent eviction, the goats let out a chorus of plaintive bleats.

"About the supplies," I started. "If we're going to be here for a while—"

"We have plenty," Begonia interrupted. "The pantry is well-stocked. We keep stores for winter—rice, pasta, beans, flour. And we have the garden, the chickens. We are surrounded by fields." She added another serving of eggs to her plate. "We will not starve."

"How long could we last? Realistically?"

She was quiet for a moment, her spoon hovering above her plate. "The winter would not be fun," she admitted. She glanced at the faces around the table, her expression serious. "But we would make it."

"I have no idea what's going to happen," I admitted. "But I'd rather plan for the worst and be pleasantly surprised."

"Very American of you," Rose interjected flatly.

"I'll take that as a compliment this one time."

She looked up from her meal with a twinkle in her eyes. "It was meant as one." She winked. "This one time."

***

By dinnertime, the courtyard was securely fenced in and the goats had all been expelled from the house. Unfortunately, the horrible little beasts were objecting to a return to their exterior status and kept finding their way back inside. Grace and William were on goat patrol and the little boy met me at the bottom of the stairs, a tiny white goat struggling in his arms.

"This one is named Bert," he told me solemnly. "He's not a good listener."

Hmm, I wondered where he'd heard that phrase.

Grace appeared behind him. "William," she barked. "Out." She pointed toward the door and the little boy stomped away, face like a thundercloud.

"Everything okay?" I asked, eyebrows raised.

Eyes following the boy as he took his small charge out to the courtyard, Grace frowned. "We get one outside and two more make it back in. This is ridiculous." She finally turned to face me, running a hand over her eyes. "I need a nap."

"Where's Darla?" I asked, as William came back empty handed.

Grace headed toward the stairs without a backward glance. "I don't think I'm cut out for parenthood, Helena," she called over her shoulder. "Tag, you're it."

Oh, hell, no.

"Grace!" I yelled up the stairs as she disappeared around the landing and William sidled up to me, eyes wide at the panic in my voice.

Okay, Helena, rein it back in, I told myself. I was a teacher for twenty years. I could definitely handle one kid. Of course, those were high schoolers, who were basically adult-sized. This one wasn't even half-cooked. And I was definitely out of practice.

"Where's your mom?"

William came even closer. "She's taking a nap," he said in his gruff little boy voice. "I didn't have any more nap in me, so I was helping Miss Grace with the goats."

"That sounds fun," I offered.

The boy shrugged. "I had fun and the goats had fun, but I don't think Miss Grace had fun."

"No," I agreed. "I don't think she did."

"Ahhh!" someone screamed behind me.

I jumped, spinning to find a small white goat standing on the front desk. I pressed a hand over my racing heart as the beast opened its mouth and emitted another very human-sounding cry. Wait, wasn't that...

"Bert!" William scolded. "Is that where you're supposed to be?" he climbed up onto the chair behind the desk to frown at the miscreant.

"How did he get back into the house?" I gasped.

William shrugged, wrapping his arms around the little goat and jumping down from the chair in a manner of which I was fairly sure his mother would not have approved.

This time I watched William put the goat outside and firmly close the door behind it. The sun had already set and someone—no doubt Jean Luc—had lit the braziers on the patio.

"Let's go figure out dinner." I offered William my hand and we headed toward the kitchen. Even the faint eau de goat that permeated the first floor couldn't disguise the lovely scents of dinner wafting our way.

Inside, Begonia and Rose were sitting at the table while Henry stood at the sink, washing his hands. He glanced over when we walked in.

"Where's Grace?" he asked, drying his hands on one of Begonia's pretty embroidered hand towels.

"Taking a well-deserved nap," I replied shortly. "And so is Darla."

"They okay?"

"No. But neither am I, so I'm not really in a position to judge." I turned to face him.

"It's never stopped you before."

Little ears were listening, so I took the high road and flipped him off.

A little plastic timer shaped like a tomato dinged on the countertop and Begonia jumped to her feet. She opened the oven and the room was suddenly full of the mouth-watering aroma of roasted chicken. Within minutes we were sitting at the table.

"May we join you?" Ashley asked from the doorway, Robert standing sullenly behind her.

"Of course, *mon cher*," Begonia magically produced two more plates and we shuffled the chairs around the table to make room.

Begonia had outdone herself once again. The roasted chicken was accompanied by root vegetables that had been caramelized to perfection and bread that was still warm from the oven.

"This is incredible," Ashley said, her eyes closed in appreciation. "Better than any restaurant."

"Now, I don't believe that. I'm sure you've been to some fancy restaurants in the states?" Begonia asked innocently.

Ashley cut her gaze to Robert before replying. "Restaurants where you needed a microscope to see your food and a second mortgage to pay the bill." Ashley stabbed a potato with more force than strictly necessary. "With weird sauces and *foam*."

"Pretentious garbage," Rose pronounced. "Give me real food any day."

"Amen," I agreed, reaching for another piece of chicken.

When the table was cleared, Begonia set several cartons of melting ice cream in the center and we all began to dig in.

"I am going to get the good wine," Rose announced. She jumped up from the table and returned a moment later with a bottle covered in dust. "From the year Jean Luc was born."

"Rose, we can't drink that," Begonia protested, aghast. "I was saving it for a special occasion!"

"The zombie apocalypse is not special?" Rose was already working the bottle open with practiced ease. The cork came free with a soft pop as we all froze.

Begonia sighed. "Oh Rose, please do not use the Zed word."

Rose poured generous glasses for each of us, the wine a deep ruby red that caught the light from the candles. I took a sip and had to close my eyes. It was exquisite—layers of dark fruit and spice, smooth and complex. It paired perfectly with the Rocky Road.

Who knew?

"Oh, my god," Ashley breathed. "That's amazing."

"My husband Eduard bought four bottles the day Jean Luc was born," Begonia said softly. "We were supposed to drink them on special occasions." She took a sip, her eyes distant. "We drank one when Jean Luc graduated university."

"I'm sorry—" I started.

"Don't be," Begonia interrupted firmly. "My *belle-mère* is correct. Life is too short and too strange to horde our pleasures." She raised her glass. "To Eduard. Who would have loved this ridiculous disaster of a day."

"To Eduard," we echoed, clinking our glasses together.

18

Thursday

I stumbled into the kitchen the next morning, desperately in need of coffee. The scene that greeted me was almost aggressively domestic—Begonia at the stove, Rose setting the table, Henry staring out the window with a cup of coffee.

"Good morning, sleeping beauty," Begonia greeted me cheerfully. "Coffee?"

"God, yes, please."

She poured me a cup and I settled into my usual chair, cradling the warm mug like a lifeline. Grace appeared a moment later, looking like she hadn't slept at all. Jean Luc and Darla followed close behind. Darla was moving more easily now that the worst of her bruises were starting to fade.

"Where's William?" she asked, glancing around.

"Goat herding," Henry said, nodding toward the window to the courtyard. "I'm keeping an eye on him. He's actually very good with them."

"My William?" Darla asked, incredulous.

Ashley appeared in the doorway, disgustingly bright-eyed and bushy-tailed. "Good morning!"

"Sit," Rose commanded, pointing to an empty chair. "Eat."

Ashley blinked but obeyed, settling into the chair beside Jean Luc, who immediately passed her the jam with a soft smile.

"Is Robert still sulking?" I asked, immediately regretting the question when everyone's expressions soured.

"Butthurt is the phrase the kids use these days," Rose said matter-of-factly around a mouthful of toast.

Ashley just shrugged and I let it go.

"Speaking of children," Begonia said dismissively, "Maybe William would like to go with us on a walk down the lane this morning to pick some figs."

"Is that safe?" Grace frowned, her hands tightening around her coffee mug.

"No," Henry said shortly. "It isn't."

I frowned at him. "We can't all just stay in the house forever."

We stared at each other for a long moment in a silent battle of wills. Finally Henry nodded.

"It's been quiet," he admitted. "But Jean Luc and I will go with you as security just in case."

"I think that sounds prudent," Darla offered quietly. "And it will do all of us good to get some fresh air."

I stood and moved to join Henry at the window. William was on his hands and knees, butting his head against the tiny white goat's. "He seems to be doing okay. All things considered."

"He doesn't really understand what's going on," Darla said. "Honestly, I don't either."

"Then it's settled!" Begonia clapped her hands together. "We will go on a foraging expedition. It will be very French. Very romantic."

"Nothing says romance like stealing fruit," I deadpanned.

"It is not stealing if no one is using them," Rose offered.

"It really doesn't work that way," I pointed out.

Rose gave a very French shrug in response. "Eh."

"Helena." Begonia waved her spatula in my direction in a threatening manner. "We must do something about your wardrobe."

I looked down at my pressed wool trousers and cashmere sweater set. "What's wrong with my wardrobe?"

"This is not a state function, *mon cher*." She set her spatula in the sink and grabbed my arm. "Come. I will find you something more appropriate."

"I don't need—"

"You absolutely do. *Allons-y!*"

I let myself be dragged upstairs, Henry's amused chuckle following us.

Begonia's rooms were exactly what I would have expected—an explosion of color and fabric and what could only be described as organized chaos. Scarves draped over every surface, jewelry spilled from ornate boxes, and clothes covered every available chair.

"Your husband was a saint," I observed.

"He was French. He appreciated beauty in all its forms." She began rifling through a massive armoire. "Ah! Perfect."

She pulled out a pair of dark blue jeans and a soft flannel shirt in shades of green.

"I can't wear your clothes—"

"Mine would be much too short. These were Eduard's," Begonia said softly. "Please. I think he would like knowing someone was getting use from them."

I took the clothes, my throat tight. "Thank you."

The jeans were a surprisingly good fit, soft from years of washing. The flannel shirt smelled faintly of cedar and lavender. I studied myself in the mirror and hardly recognized the woman looking back. No pressed slacks, no carefully coordinated separates. Just jeans and flannel and hair that hadn't seen a blow dryer in a week.

Dear lord. Had it only been a week?

"Magnifique!" Begonia declared. "You look like a real person!"

"Real people don't wear dress pants?" I asked dubiously.

"You know what I mean." She linked her arm through mine. "Come. Let us scandalize Henry with your casual wear."

We descended the stairs to find everyone gathered in the lobby, even Robert. Standing near the door, Jean Luc had his father's old hunting rifle resting on his shoulder. Grace stood beside him, fussing with a collection of baskets. William was explaining to Darla why he absolutely needed to bring Bert on the expedition.

"You cannot bring the goat," Darla was saying flatly.

William's lower lip trembled dangerously but Darla stood firm.

Henry looked up and whatever he'd been about to say died on his lips. His gaze traveled from my denim-clad legs up to my loose hair, his expression shifting into something I couldn't quite read.

"What?" I asked aggressively, daring him to mock my new wardrobe.

"You look good," he said simply, eyebrows rising.

I narrowed my eyes at him, but let it pass.

We set off down the road—sans goat—armed with baskets, bags, and the kind of determined optimism that only came from denial. William held Darla's hand, mood restored, skipping along and asking questions about everything we passed.

"What's that flower called? Why don't goats have fingers? Why is the sky so blue here? It isn't this blue at home, is it? Where did all of the clouds go? Can we get a goat for at home?"

Darla answered each question with the patience of a saint.

Henry and I walked near the back of the group, close enough to the others to stay connected but with enough distance for privacy.

"You doing okay?" he asked quietly.

"No," I said with a smile. "You?"

He chuckled. "Nope."

We walked in companionable silence for a while, the morning sun warm on our backs. Ahead, Begonia was gesticulating wildly while telling some story that had Jean Luc shaking his head in what looked like fond exasperation. Ashley walked beside him, smiling at their antics.

As we approached the fig trees William's excitement reached a fever pitch. He bounced on his toes, his gruff little voice rising in volume.

"Can I pick one? Why is it sticky? Why does it have a butt?"

"It's sticky because you squished it. And figs don't have butts," Darla said, shaking her head.

"Look!" He pointed to the fig's distinctive shape. "See? Butt."

"He's not wrong," Rose observed, appearing at my elbow. "Figs do look like they have little butts."

"Butts are for pooping," the little boy announced gravely.

"Thank you for that image," I said. "I'll never eat one again without thinking about it."

"You're welcome," he responded brightly.

Jean Luc demonstrated the proper way to pick a fig—a gentle twist to release them from the branch without damaging the fruit. William watched intently, then proceeded to ignore all instructions and just yank them off like he was picking apples.

"Gently, William," Darla corrected.

"But it's faster this way!"

"Faster isn't always better, honey."

"Miss Rose does it fast." He pointed accusingly at Rose, who was indeed just pulling figs off with brute force.

"Miss Rose can do it however she wants because everyone is afraid to tell her otherwise," I whispered.

We filled our baskets with figs, the fruit heavy and sweet-smelling. William discovered that if you squeezed them just right, they made a satisfying squelching sound, which led to approximately twelve figs being sacrificed to science before Darla confiscated the rest.

"Is that broccoli?" Grace pointed into the field behind the fig trees.

We crouched down to see behind the trees and sure enough, a massive field of broccoli stretched before us, the plants heavy with dark green crowns.

"Jackpot," Henry said.

"Oh, no," William groaned. "Not broccoli."

"What's wrong with broccoli?" I asked.

The little boy stepped closer and cupped his hands around his mouth and whisper-screamed into my face, "It makes me fart. A lot."

"I'm really sorry I asked," I admitted.

"Jean Luc," Begonia called. "Run back to the house. Grab some more knives and fetch the car! We'll fill it up!"

Jean Luc jogged back toward the inn while the rest of us waded into the field. The broccoli plants were massive, their crowns the size of my head.

"The boy has a point," Rose said. "Broccoli makes me very gassy as well."

"Oh, my god," Ashley breathed, her shoulders shaking with suppressed laughter.

Jean Luc returned with the Fiat and we began loading every inch of the little car. By early afternoon we'd harvested enough broccoli to feed a small army. Jean Luc wedged himself behind the wheel and drove back slowly. The rest of us trudged back to the inn in the little car's wake, like victorious soldiers returning from battle.

Begonia was in heaven. "Broccoli soup, broccoli quiche, roasted broccoli, broccoli pasta—"

"Please stop," William begged.

"I will make broccoli gratin," Begonia continued, ignoring him. "You will love it, *petit homme.*"

"No, I won't," the little boy said sadly, hanging his head.

Back at the inn, we unloaded everything into the kitchen. Broccoli covered every surface, green crowns piled in precarious towers. The fat white cat took one look at the vegetable invasion and fled, his tail bristling.

"I'll start blanching," Ashley offered, rolling up her sleeves.

"I'll help," Jean Luc said immediately, moving to her side.

They stood at the sink together, working in easy harmony. Jean Luc trimmed the broccoli and passed it to Ashley, who blanched it in boiling water before plunging it into an ice bath.

William appeared at my elbow, sticky with fig juice and smelling like dirt. "Miss Helena?"

"Yes, William?"

"Can I have a fig for Bert?"

I looked down at his earnest little face, streaked with dirt and hope. "Sure. But only one, okay? We need the rest for us."

"Okay!" He grabbed a fig from the basket and ran outside, shouting. "Bert! I have a surprise for you!"

Darla appeared beside me, watching through the window as William carefully offered the fig to the little goat. Bert sniffed it suspiciously before snatching it from the boy's hand and making a run for it.

Henry joined us at the window, his presence warm and solid beside me. Outside, William was now chasing the little goat around the fenced courtyard, complete with sound effects.

"This is insane," I said conversationally.

"Completely," Henry agreed.

Henry's shoulder brushed mine. We stood there for a moment, watching William and Bert through the window.

"Helena!" Begonia called from the kitchen. "Come help me decide which wine pairs best with broccoli soup!"

"That's my cue," I said, but I didn't move right away.

"Helena," he said quietly.

"Yeah?"

"You look good in jeans."

My face was suddenly warm. "Thanks."

I bumped his shoulder gently with mine and turned away. Grace was slipping out of the kitchen as I walked in to find Begonia holding up two bottles of wine and debating their merits with Rose.

"The Côtes du Rhône," Rose was insisting. "The Bordeaux is too heavy."

"The Bordeaux has more body—"

"Which is exactly why it's too heavy for vegetables!"

I looked around the kitchen—at Ashley and Jean Luc working side by side, at Begonia and Rose bickering over wine, at Darla sitting at the table, gazing into the distance.

"You know what?" I said, grabbing a wine glass. "Pour them both. Let's do a comparison."

Begonia's face lit up. "Now you are thinking like a French woman!"

"Don't get too excited. I'm still wearing sensible underwear."

"We will work on that next," Rose promised.

"We will not," I assured her.

19

Thursday Night

For dinner there was in fact roasted broccoli and broccoli soup, along with the last of the chicken and fig tarts that could have graced the table of any restaurant in Paris.

We were once more outside, sitting around the big table in the courtyard with candles and ceramic chimineas blazing merrily around us, creating a little warm oasis in the cool night air. The goats were sleeping in piles in the corners of the fenced terrace as everyone moved to the table, sliding into their chairs.

I glanced around at the now familiar faces and frowned. "Where's Grace?"

"She had a headache earlier and went upstairs to take a nap in her room," Begonia said, passing me a bowl of broccoli soup.

I frowned. "Maybe I should go check on her," I murmured as a scream cut through the night.

We all froze.

Another scream, followed by the sound of breaking glass from above us.

Henry was on his feet before the glass finished shattering, his hand already on his weapon. I stood so fast my chair tipped backward.

"One of them got in," I gasped in horror.

We ran through the french doors and sprinted up the stairs, Henry and Jean Luc taking the lead. Another crash sounded as they made the landing.

"Grace's room." I pointed, my heart hammering against my ribs, my mind cycling through terrible possibilities.

Henry paused at Grace's door, his weapon drawn. He raised a foot and kicked, the door swinging open. Inside the darkened room, someone was sobbing—great heaving gasps between screams.

Henry stood frozen in the doorway and I pushed past him and stopped dead.

Grace was alone.

The meager light streaming in through the open window illuminated the mattress, half off the bed, and the sheets tangled on the floor. The curtains had been torn from the window. Books—Grace's beloved books that she traveled with everywhere—were scattered across the floor, their pages torn out and crumpled.

And Grace stood in the center of it all, her hair wild around her face. She was holding a large porcelain lamp in her hands, the shade hanging askew and the cord trailing across the room to where it was still plugged into the wall.

"Grace?" I took a step forward.

She spun toward me, and the moonlight washed her face in a silvery glow. Her mouth was twisted with rage, her eyes streaming tears down her cheeks.

"Everything is wrong!" she screamed, her voice raw. She jerked the lamp to pop the cord free.

Then she hurled the lamp at my head.

I ducked. The lamp sailed past me and shattered against the wall, shards spraying the room.

"Grace!"

She rounded the bed, her movements jerky and uncoordinated, and lifted the matching lamp from the other small bedside table, raising it over her head.

"Everybody back," Henry ordered, his voice sharp.

I stood there, staring at Grace—Grace, who was always so composed, so careful, so kind—as she shattered the second lamp against the wall. Then she gripped the small table it had been sitting on and raised it over her head with an expression of absolute fury. Turning, Grace arched her back and hurled the table at the window.

We all lurched away as glass shattered across the room, the window frame splintering.

"We need to restrain her," Robert said from behind me. He'd appeared in the doorway, his face pale. "Before she kills someone."

"Wait—" Henry started.

But Robert was already moving forward, reaching for Grace's arms.

Grace screamed into his face, her voice hoarse, barely recognizable. She twisted away from him, her elbow catching him in the chest.

"You little—" Robert grabbed her wrist, yanking her toward him.

"Don't!" I lunged forward, but Henry grabbed my shoulders and pulled me away.

Across the room, Robert and Grace were a mess of limbs and curses in the dim light.

Grace fought like a wild animal, all nails and teeth and desperate strength. She caught Robert across the face with her free hand, leaving red welts on his cheek.

He swore and shoved her backward.

Hard.

Grace stumbled, her feet tangling in the bed sheets strewn across the floor. She fell backward, her arms windmilling as she tried to catch her balance.

The back of her thighs hit the windowsill.

For one horrible moment, she teetered there, half in and half out of the window.

"No!" I screamed.

Grace tipped backward and disappeared.

The awful thump she made when she hit the ground below would haunt me for the rest of my life.

***

I heard that sound again when Henry and Jean Luc tipped her body into Rose's well. I'd argued long and hard against it, but at the end of the day there were no other good options. If I were twenty years younger I might have tried to dig her a real grave myself. I think I could have bullied the others into helping me, but the practical part of my brain wouldn't let me.

So Grace joined the two unidentified men and an indeterminate number of lascivious Nazi soldiers in the bottom of Rose's well. And I buried that thump in the back of my mind with the rattle of John's last breath and the chill of his paper thin skin over the bones of his fingers as his hand grew still in mine.

"I won't forget, Grace," I murmured. "I won't forget."

The cat had followed our sad little procession and jumped up to the stone edge. He looked down into the darkness that had swallowed Grace as we all stood in silence for another long moment. Then warm hands were turning me back toward the inn and I focused on the circle of light Rose's flashlight made on the grass. I followed the light without thought, moving toward it as it moved forward, like falling into a bottomless pit.

"Are you okay?" Begonia's voice was soft beside me, her accent thicker than usual.

"Why does everyone keep asking me that?"

Ahead of me William pulled against his mother's grip. "Mama, you're hurting me."

"Quiet, William" Darla said, her voice flat.

The boy's lower lip trembled but he went silent.

Up ahead, Jean Luc led the way with his old hunting rifle. Behind, Henry and Ashley stumbled through the damp grass. Robert brought up the rear, silently fingering the scratches on his face.

We were a motley crew and far less than Grace deserved.

20

Friday

It rained the next day, and I didn't leave my room. The sky never really brightened past a dull gray, but it had to be afternoon when Begonia brought me a tray. I stared at the cooling broccoli soup and fresh bread, and left it on the desk untouched.

I sat in my bed as the room grew dark. At some point Henry arrived with candles and a book. He claimed the plush chair beside the bed and read his book, not trying to talk.

Smart man.

There was one thought that circled my mind like a vulture, picking at the corpse of my composure. I'd brought Grace here. I'd insisted she come despite her protests that she needed to go back to DC.

Eventually Henry left me to go to bed and I stared at the ceiling until the room began to lighten again. At some point I must have dozed off because I woke suddenly, unable to breathe.

Is this a heart attack? I wondered mildly, not terribly concerned either way.

But the beast on my chest was not metaphorical, it was all too physical. And white. And fluffy. I rolled to my side, dislodging the cat and gasped.

"How did you even get in here?" My voice was hoarse from disuse and my mouth sour.

As the cat disappeared over the side of the bed, I pushed myself up against the pillows and I ran my hands over my head. My hair was greasy and flat against my skull.

I was considering a shower when there was a knock at the door.

"Helena?" Begonia's voice, muffled through the wood. "I am coming in, *mon cher.*"

"Don't," I said.

The door opened anyway because boundaries are apparently for losers.

Begonia swept in wearing a caftan in shades of pink and gold that seemed aggressively cheerful given the circumstances. She set another tray on the desk, tutting over the intact meal from the previous night.

"This is enough," she said firmly, sitting on the edge of the bed, her weight making the mattress dip. "I understand grief, but you are behaving like a child."

"Fuck off," I drawled.

"Children do not get to be left alone. They get lectures and vegetables." She yanked the covers down, exposing me to the dim light filtering through the curtains. "Sit up."

"No," I clung to the blanket, the cool air shocking against my skin.

"Sit. Up."

Something in her tone made me comply despite myself. I struggled upright, my unwashed hair falling into my eyes. I probably looked like something that had crawled out of a bog.

Begonia's expression softened. "Oh, *chérie*. You look terrible."

"Thank you. That's very helpful."

"It is honest." She reached out, tucking a strand of greasy hair behind my ear. "Grace would not want this."

"Grace doesn't want anything, because Grace is dead." The words came out flat, emotionless. I'd said them so many times in my head that they'd lost their power to hurt. Now they were just fact.

"This was not your fault, Helena," Begonia pointed out gently.

"I brought her here."

"You did not infect her."

"I might as well have." I looked down at my hands. "If I hadn't insisted she come, if I'd let her go back to DC—"

"Then she would be dead there instead of here," Begonia interrupted.

"You don't know that," I protested.

"Neither do you," Begonia pointed out. "At least here she was not alone."

"She was alone," I said bitterly. "She fell out a window and broke her neck and we threw her in a fucking well with a bunch of Nazis."

"Helena—"

"I know you mean well, Begonia." I lay back down, pulling the covers up. "But, please. Just go."

She was quiet for a long moment. Then she stood, the bed creaking slightly with the shift in weight.

"You must eat something," she said. "I will be back. And next time I will bring Rose, and she will not be so gentle."

With that threat, the door closed with a soft click.

***

"Helena!" Grace's voice was high with panic as she tipped backwards. "Helena, help me!"

The fall seemed to last forever. Grace's eyes locked on mine, terrified and betrayed, as she fell away from me. Away and away and away until she was just a small figure tumbling through the air.

Then came the thump.

I jerked awake, my heart hammering against my ribs hard enough to hurt. The bedsheets were soaked with sweat, twisted around my legs like they were trying to hold me down. For a moment I couldn't breathe, couldn't think, couldn't do anything but lie there in the darkness and try to remember that it was just a dream.

Except it wasn't.

I dislodged the cat again from my chest and kicked free of the sheets, stumbling out of bed. My legs were shaky, my head spinning. The room was cool, but the air was thick and suffocating.

I needed to wash the dream off, wash away the image of Grace's terrified face as she fell.

The bathroom was dark, the overhead light still useless. It took me three tries to light a candle, but soon a dancing yellow glow threw shadows across the walls. I turned on the shower, waiting for the water to heat, and caught sight of myself in the mirror.

Jesus Christ.

Begonia had been kind. I looked like a corpse that had been left out in the rain. My hair was a rat's nest, my face was pale and drawn, and my eyes were sunken and bruised.

"You are a goddamn mess, Helena," I told my reflection.

She didn't argue.

When I stepped into the shower the water was hot enough to hurt, and I turned my face into the spray, letting it pound against my skin.

What in the hell was wrong with me?

The question rose up unbidden, sharp and insistent. People were dead, dying, and I was sitting around drinking wine and making jokes like this was all some extended vacation.

Like it wasn't the end of the fucking world.

I pressed my forehead against the cool tile, letting the water run down my back. I'd been treating this whole thing like an adventure. A vacation.

I should have been terrified. And I was, in a distant, abstract way. But underneath the fear was something else. Something that felt almost like relief.

No more press conferences. No more political theater. No more smiling for cameras or biting my tongue during meetings with people I despised.

I'd been having fun. I'd been enjoying the apocalypse.

And now Grace was dead.

I laughed, the sound harsh and bitter in the small bathroom. "You're losing it, Barrett. You're actually losing it."

I shut off the water and stood there dripping in the candlelight until my skin was covered in goosebumps. I wrapped myself in the big, fluffy robe hanging from the back of the door, and stared at my reflection again.

I looked marginally more human. Still tired. Still grief-stricken. But human.

"Grace deserved better," I told my reflection.

She stared back in agreement, hollow-eyed and silent.

I was halfway across the bedroom, heading toward the bed and another twelve hours of wallowing, when someone knocked at the door. Again.

"Begonia, I really don't—"

"It's me," Henry's voice cut through my threat.

I froze, one hand on the bedpost.

"Can I come in?"

"I'm not dressed," I burst out as the door opened.

Henry froze with the door half open and his gaze swept me up and down. "You're in a robe. I've seen you in less." A pause. "That came out wrong."

Despite everything, a laugh bubbled up in my chest. It felt rusty, unused, but it was there. "You're an idiot."

Henry's hair was rumpled like he'd been running his hands through it. His shirt was untucked, his jaw shadowed with stubble. He looked tired. We all probably looked tired.

"You look like shit," he said.

"You really know how to sweet talk a girl."

His mouth twitched. Not quite a smile, but close. "Come downstairs and have breakfast with us," he ordered. "No more hiding."

"I haven't been hiding."

"What would you call it?" Henry took a few steps into the room.

"Strategic withdrawal." I crossed my arms.

He came closer, his gaze steady on mine. "You have to stop punishing yourself."

"I'm not—"

"Grace's death wasn't your fault."

The words hit like a physical blow.

"You've been talking to Begonia." I turned away, moving to the french doors. I flung them open, trying to get air into my lungs. Outside, the sun hung low in the horizon and the sky was a perfect cloudless blue, light and delicate, stretching out over the fields.

Henry stood close behind me. "You didn't infect her. You didn't push her out the window."

"I made her come here."

"You didn't." His voice was gentle but firm. "Grace was so excited for this trip. She was so happy you were finally taking a break." He paused. "She was happy to be here, Helena. Even with everything that's happened, I think she would have made the same choice."

"You can't know that," I said quietly.

"No," he admitted. "But I knew Grace. And I know you. And I know that hiding in this room isn't going to bring her back."

"I'm not trying to bring her back." I turned to face him. "I'm just—" I stopped, the words catching in my throat.

"You're what?"

"I'm tired, Henry." The admission came out broken. "I'm so fucking tired. John got sick and I took care of him and watched him fade away piece by piece. Then he died and I couldn't even grieve properly because everyone needed me to be strong, to carry on his legacy, to smile for the cameras." My voice rose. "I finally get fired, I finally get to be free, and the whole goddamn world ends!"

"Helena—"

"And now Grace is dead and Jacob and god knows how many other people. I can't keep pretending everything is going to be fine."

"No one's asking you to pretend." Henry's voice was calm, steady. "We're all scared. We're all grieving. But hiding in here isn't helping anyone."

"I don't care about helping anyone!" The words exploded out of me. "I don't care about being strong or being a leader or being whatever the fuck everyone needs me to be. I'm done!"

The silence that followed was deafening.

Henry didn't move, didn't speak, just stood there watching me with those steady eyes.

Finally, quietly, he said: "Then what about what I need?"

I blinked. "What?"

"What about what I need, Helena?" He took a step closer. "Because I need you."

"You don't need me. You're perfectly capable—"

"I came here for you." The words came out rough, urgent. "I quit, Helena. I walked away from twenty years of service because I wasn't leaving you in Paris alone."

The air left my lungs in a rush. "What?"

"I was supposed to go back to DC with the rest of your security detail. Report back immediately or face termination." His jaw tightened. "I told them to shove their termination up their ass."

"Henry—"

"So yeah, I need you to not give up." He moved closer, close enough that I could see the exhaustion in his eyes, the lines bracketing his mouth.

Guilt crashed over me in a wave. "Jesus, Henry. That just makes me feel worse."

His lips quirked up into a small smile. "No pressure." He reached out, his hand closing around mine. His fingers were warm, solid, real. "But it would be really great if you would come downstairs and have some coffee."

I looked down at his hand, at the familiar scars on his knuckles, at the watch he'd worn every day for the ten years I'd known him.

"I don't know if I can," I whispered.

"You absolutely can. I have zero doubt." His thumb moved against my pulse point, gentle. "You're the strongest person I know."

"I'm really not."

"You took care of your husband while he forgot who you were. You kept working, kept smiling, kept functioning while your whole world fell apart." His voice softened. "You can do this."

"That was different."

"How?"

"Because John needed me. I had a purpose."

"And you don't think these people need you?" Henry asked. "You don't think I need you?"

The question hung in the air between us.

"I'm scared," I admitted. "I'm scared that if I go downstairs and try to be normal, I'll fall apart. And if I fall apart, everyone else will too."

"Then we'll fall apart together." Henry's voice was gentle but firm. "That's what people do. They fall apart and they put themselves back together and they keep going."

"Very poetic."

"I have my moments."

I turned to face him. "I can't promise I won't be a mess."

"I'm not asking you to be perfect. I'm just asking you to show up."

Show up. As if it were that simple.

Except maybe it was.

I looked at Henry—solid, steady, impossibly patient Henry—and felt something in my chest loosen. Just a fraction.

"Give me ten minutes," I said.

He released his breath, his smile reaching his eyes. "Ten minutes. I'll tell Begonia to make extra coffee."

He moved toward the door, then paused. "Helena?"

"Yeah?"

"For what it's worth—I'm glad we're here. Even with everything that's happened. I'm glad I'm here with you."

The door closed behind him before I could respond.

I stood there in the growing light, my throat tight, my eyes burning with tears I'd been holding back.

"Goddammit, Henry," I whispered.

21
Saturday Morning

The kitchen smelled like coffee and bread, and for a moment I just stood in the doorway, letting the normalcy of it wash over me.

Begonia was at the stove, today's dress a riot of oranges and reds that hurt to look at pre-coffee. Rose sat at the table, already working her way through a piece of toast with jam. Henry leaned against the counter, a steaming mug in his hands, and when he saw me, his expression softened.

"You came," he said simply.

"Don't make a big deal out of it."

"Wouldn't dream of it." But his mouth quirked at the corner.

Begonia turned, her face lighting up like a Christmas tree. "Helena!" She pulled me into a brief but fierce hug before ushering me into the chair across from Rose.

A cup appeared in front of me, steam rising in gentle spirals. I wrapped both hands around it, letting the warmth seep into my palms.

"You look terrible," Rose observed, studying me over the rim of her own cup.

"Your compliments are always so heartwarming."

"I am very old. I don't have time to beat around the bush."

Ashley appeared in the doorway, her hair pulled back in a messy ponytail, her face drawn. "Good morning," she said quietly, sliding into the seat beside me.

"How's Robert?" Begonia asked, setting a plate of croissants on the table.

Ashley's expression shuttered. "He won't come out of his room."

"Has he said anything?" Henry asked.

"Just that this is all my fault for booking this place." Ashley's laugh was bitter. "Apparently if we'd stayed in Paris, none of this would have happened."

"Yes," Rose said dryly. "Because the city is famously immune from disease and riots."

"Logic isn't his strong suit right now." Ashley tore a piece off her croissant without eating it.

We sat in silence for a moment, the weight of everything unsaid pressing down on the table like a physical presence.

"Speaking of people hiding in their rooms," I said, looking around. "Where's Darla? And William?"

Begonia frowned as she set a plate of steaming scrambled eggs and broccoli on the table before me. "I have not seen them this morning. I assumed they were sleeping late."

"That kid's usually up with the roosters, terrorizing the goats," Henry said, his tone sharpening slightly.

A trickle of unease ran down my spine and I set my coffee on the table. "Maybe I should go check on them."

Begonia waved toward my plate. "Your food will get cold, *mon ami*."

Jean Luc came through the back door, a basket of eggs in his hands. His face was flushed from the cool morning air.

"Bonjour! The chickens are very productive this morning." He set the basket on the counter. "We will have omelets for days."

"Jean Luc," Begonia said. "Would you mind checking on Darla and William?"

"Of course, *Maman*." He moved toward the door with a youthful vigor that was exhausting.

I sighed as I filled my fork. "So eggs and broccoli for breakfast, lunch, and dinner?"

Begonia laughed and waved a finger in my direction. "Eat, *mon cher*. It may not be up to Parisian standards, but it is good, healthy food."

I swallowed the bite in my mouth and gave her a wan smile. "It's delicious." I picked up my cup to take another sip of the rich, dark roast and froze as an unpleasant thought occurred to me. "Begonia?"

She turned at the concern in my voice. "*Qui?*"

"How much coffee do we have left?"

The horrified silence in the kitchen was disturbed by the thundering of Jean Luc's footsteps back down the main staircase. He burst into the kitchen, his face pale.

"They are not there," he said, breathing hard. "And the room—it is destroyed."

We all stood at once, chairs scraping against the floor.

"What do you mean?" Begonia demanded.

"Like Grace's room. Everything is broken, thrown around. The window is open." Jean Luc ran a hand through his hair. "They are not in the room."

Ice flooded my veins. "Show us."

We followed him up the stairs, Henry already pulling ahead. The Hibiscus Room was at the end of the hall, its door hanging open. Henry stopped in the doorway, blocking it with his body.

"Henry, move," I said.

He turned to look at me, his expression grave. Then he stepped aside.

The room was unrecognizable. The mattress was halfway off the bed, sheets torn and scattered. Clothes had been pulled from the dresser and thrown across the floor. The curtains hung in tatters. And the window—the window was wide open, the screen torn out and lying crumpled on the floor.

"Oh god," Ashley whispered behind me.

My feet took me to the window, my heart hammering in my ears as I approached. Below, in the garden, there was disturbed earth and trampled flowers. But no bodies. No blood.

"They're not here," I said. My mind was racing, connecting dots I didn't want to connect. "We need to search the property."

"You think Darla was infected, went crazy," Henry said. It wasn't a question.

"We have to assume that." I turned to face the room. "We need to find them. Now."

"What about William?" Ashley's voice cracked. "If Darla's infected—"

"Don't," I cut her off, unable to voice the terrible possibilities forming in my mind.

We split up quickly. Jean Luc grabbed his father's hunting rifle, his expression grim. Ashley moved to his side without being asked.

"We will search the outbuildings," Jean Luc said. "The barn, the goat shed, the storage areas."

Henry nodded. "Begonia, Helena, and I will take the gardens and the fields. Rose, you stay here in case they come back."

Nobody argued.

Outside, the morning was breathtaking. The sky was blue and the air scented with lavender and rosemary. Birds sang and goats bleated as we headed toward the rear of the property.

"Where would she go?" Begonia asked, wringing her hands as we walked. "If she was confused, disoriented—"

"What's the path of least resistance?" Henry asked. "If she weren't thinking straight and just ran." He'd drawn his weapon, holding it low but ready. His eyes scanned constantly, cataloging every shadow, every movement.

"This way." Begonia led us toward the back of the garden, her caftan streaming behind her. "The path is wide and slightly downhill."

We followed her through the neat rows of vegetables, past the herb garden, toward the wilder areas at the edge of the property. My eyes searched everywhere—behind trees, under bushes, anywhere a small boy or a desperate woman might hide.

"Darla!" I called. "Darla, if you can hear me, we want to help you!"

Silence. Just the wind in the trees and the distant bleating of the goats.

"William!" Begonia's voice was louder, more urgent. "*Petit homme*, where are you?"

"Maybe they're not—" I started.

There was a rustling up ahead and we all froze.

"There," Henry said, pointing toward a dense thicket of bushes about fifty yards ahead. "Stay behind me."

We crept closer, my heart hammering so hard I could feel it in my throat. The bush shook violently. Branches snapped.

William emerged from the foliage and ran toward us.

My heart leapt in relief. He was dirty and crying, but he was alive. "William!"

His head swiveled toward me, golden brown curls bobbing.

The breath ran from my lungs as my heart hit the ground. "Oh, no," I said softly.

William's eyes were red and streaming, tears cutting tracks through the dirt on his face. His mouth hung open, a low growl pouring out of him. His hands were bleeding, fingers arched into tiny claws tipped with torn, broken nails.

There was no recognition in his face. Just rage.

"Helena!" Henry yelled, moving forward, gun in hand.

I threw out my arm, putting myself between Henry and William. "Put your god damn gun away!"

William was fast—faster than he should have been—but he was still a six-year-old boy. I planted my hand on the top of his head and he stopped in his tracks. He flailed from a safe distance, small hands raking at the air, mouth open and growling.

"I wasn't going to shoot him," Henry muttered, holstering his weapon.

"What do we do?" Begonia's voice was high with panic. "We cannot hurt him, he is just a *bébé*, but—"

"We need to restrain him," Henry said bluntly, moving behind William. "We need rope."

"Here. Use this," Begonia said, unraveling the red and orange scarf from her neck. "This is silk. It is strong."

Henry grabbed one of the boy's arms and twisted it behind his back as William growled and thrashed.

"Don't hurt him!" I yelled, my hand still buried in William's curls.

The boy snapped at Henry, who snagged his other wrist and began tying them together with Begonia's scarf.

"Don't hurt *him*?" Henry scoffed. "Nice to see you're not worried about me."

I met Henry's gaze under his furrowed brow. "He's just a little boy," I said softly while the little boy in question growled and thrashed between us.

"What's your plan, Helena?" Henry asked, lifting the boy up by his bound arms. William twisted his little body this way and that, snapping his teeth.

What I really wanted to do was to sink into the grass and cry, but I knew that wasn't an option.

"This is bad," Begonia said. "We will all become infected."

I shook my head. "I don't think so," I told her. "Let's get him back to the house."

Begonia's hand found mine, squeezing tight. "And then what?"

"I have no fucking idea," I admitted.

22

Saturday Afternoon

The trip back to the house was like hauling a sack of angry, feral cats up a mountain. Granted, William wasn't that heavy and the incline was more a gentle rise than a mountain, but still. It wasn't fun. By the time the house came into view, we were all tired and irritable.

"Stop wiggling," Henry grunted, adjusting his grip on the boy's shoulders.

William responded by craning his neck to try to bite Henry's arm.

"Jesus Christ," Henry muttered, jerking back.

I was supporting William's waist, which kept his gnashing teeth at a safe distance. Begonia was holding his feet, bound with Henry's belt, and murmuring French curses under her breath.

"Almost there." I sighed in relief at the sight of the inn's tile roof.

The courtyard was still fenced off for the goats, so we had to walk around to the front door. Begonia kicked at it and yelled, "Rose! *Ouvrez la porte!*"

The door swung open, but it was Robert who stood there, his face pale, the scratches from his scuffle with Grace harsh red lines across his cheek.

"What the hell is going on?" he demanded, staring at William.

"Move," I said flatly.

"What's wrong with that kid?" Robert placed a hand on either side of the frame, blocking the doorway with his body. "Holy crap. He's infected!"

"Please move out of the way, *monsieur*," Begonia said, her voice shaking with exhaustion.

"He's infected," Robert repeated. His eyes were wild, darting between William's snarling face and each of us. "You can't bring him in here."

Begonia straightened her back. "This is my house, *monsieur*. Move out of the way."

"No." Robert crossed his arms. "I'm not letting you kill us all because you have some misguided maternal instinct."

White-hot rage flooded through me and I craned my neck around Begonia to narrow my eyes at him. "Robert, move your ass. Now."

"Make me."

William chose that moment to let out an ear-splitting shriek that made us all wince. My arms were shaking with exertion, my shoulders screaming in protest.

"You're all insane!" Robert leaned into Begonia's face. "Use your brain. We can't—"

The clang of heavy cast iron meeting the back of his thick skull cut off whatever else Robert was going to say. His eyes rolled up into his head like a cartoon character and he crumpled to the floor in a heap.

Behind him, Rose stood holding Begonia's frying pan, her expression utterly serene.

"Bring the boy inside," she said calmly, stepping over Robert's prone form.

I loved that woman.

We hauled William through the doorway, stepping over Robert without a second glance.

Ashley and Jean Luc appeared in the kitchen doorway.

"You found him!" she cried, rushing toward us. She stuttered to a stop when she noticed Robert's body on the floor.

"Is he—" she started.

"Leave him," Rose said dismissively.

We wrestled William up the stairs, his small body fighting us every step of the way. By the time we reached Darla's room my arms felt like overcooked noodles and I was drenched in sweat.

I'd forgotten what a mess it was in here, but Ashley and Jean Luc sprang into action. Between the two of them they maneuvered the mattress back on the bed in under a minute.

As soon as it was in place we lowered him onto the soft surface and he immediately tried to roll off. Henry caught him, pressing the boy back down while I looked around desperately for something to secure him with.

"The sheets," Begonia said, gathering them from where they were strewn across the floor. "We can tie him down."

"Tie him to the bed?" I protested.

"Don't get squeamish now, Hellcat," Henry cautioned through gritted teeth as William nearly twisted out of his grasp. "This is going to get worse before it gets better."

And it did.

We worked quickly, using the sheets to secure William's legs to the bedposts. His hands were still bound with Begonia's scarf, but I added another sheet around his chest and the mattress for good measure. It wasn't pretty, but it would keep him from hurting himself.

Or us.

William thrashed against the restraints, his face twisted with rage and fever. Tears streamed from his red-rimmed eyes, and that horrible keening sound poured from his throat.

"*Mon dieu*," Begonia whispered, her hand over her mouth.

"We need to keep him hydrated," I said, forcing my brain into problem-solving mode. "And we need to figure out how this thing spreads."

"Bodily fluids?" Henry suggested. "Blood, saliva?"

"What if it's airborne?" Ashley asked from the other side of the bed, her arms wrapped around herself.

"If it's airborne, we've already been exposed," I admitted.

"I will gather supplies," Begonia said, already heading for the door. "Towels. Water. We will need lots of water."

I moved closer to the bed, studying William. Up close, I could see the fever flush on his cheeks, the way his chest heaved with each breath. His eyes tracked me, but there was no recognition there. There was something more than aggression, though.

Pain.

"Hey, buddy," I said softly. "We're going to take care of you, okay? You're going to be fine."

He snarled at me.

"Yeah," I agreed.

23

Sunday

We sat down the next morning and came up with a schedule. Each of us took turns watching William, trying to get water into him with a damp cloth pressed to his lips.

Begonia's oven mitts were ridiculous—bright red with little roosters on them—but they worked. William's teeth couldn't penetrate the thick quilted fabric when he tried to bite, which he did. Frequently.

"Come on, buddy," I murmured as I dripped water onto his dry lips. "Just a little more." I spoke in a low, steady voice, as William's head thrashed from side to side, his growl rising in pitch. His red-rimmed eyes tracked my movements with predatory focus.

"I know you're in there somewhere," I continued, my voice steady despite the exhaustion making my hands shake. "I know you're scared and confused and everything hurts. But we're going to get through this together."

He lunged forward as far as the restraints would allow, teeth snapping.

"Or you're going to eat my face."

Behind me, the door opened and Begonia entered carrying a fresh basin of water. She'd changed into a navy blue caftan, the most somber color I'd seen her in to date.

"Any change?" she asked, setting the basin on the bedside table.

"He's tried to bite me seventeen times in the last hour," I reported. "So, no."

"*Merde*." She turned, smoothing down her caftan. "I will make you food. You must eat something."

"I'm not hungry."

"I do not care." She paused at the door, her hand on the frame. "Thank you. For not giving up on him."

"Any word on Darla?" I asked quietly.

Begonia shook her head, her expression grieving. "There is no trace of her."

After Begonia left, I returned to my vigil as the afternoon light shifted across the room. William's growling subsided to a low, constant rumble that set my teeth on edge.

The door opened again, this time admitting Rose with a tray bearing soup and bread.

"You look like death," she announced, setting the tray on the dresser.

"Your bedside manner could use some work."

"I am not at your bedside. I am at his." She moved closer to William, studying him with the clinical detachment of someone who'd seen far too much suffering. "He is not improving."

"It's only been one day."

Rose's expression was grave. "Helena, I understand your desire to help. But sometimes the kindest thing—"

"Is not giving up on a six-year-old child," I interrupted, my voice sharper than I'd intended. "He's not a rabid dog, Rose. He's a little boy."

"A little boy who would tear out your throat if given the chance."

"Then it's a good thing he's tied down."

Rose sighed, a sound that seemed to carry the weight of decades. "You are going to break your own heart, *chérie*."

"Probably," I admitted. "But it's my heart to break."

She was quiet for a moment, her gaze moving between William and me. Finally, she nodded. "Then I will help you break it. What do you need?"

The tension in my shoulders eased slightly. "More water. Clean cloths."

Rose nodded and her mouth twitched in what might have been approval. "You are either very brave or very stupid."

"Two things can be true."

"In my experience, they often are." She moved toward the door, then paused. Her eyes found mine. "I do understand."

"I have to try," I said quietly.

"Yes," she agreed. "You do."

After she left, I forced myself to eat the soup. It was rich and warming, with that perfect balance of flavors that Begonia somehow achieved even with limited ingredients. The bread was crusty and fresh, and I ate that too, mechanically chewing while William growled and thrashed.

"You're missing out," I told him. "This soup is amazing."

The afternoon bled into evening. Ashley brought fresh water and took away the soiled cloths. Jean Luc appeared with a stack of clean towels and an update on the search.

There was still no sign of Darla. Henry came and went, his expression growing more concerned each time he checked on me.

"You need to sleep," he said during his fourth visit. "You've been up here for over twenty-four hours."

"I'm fine."

"You're not fine. You're exhausted."

"I'll sleep when I'm dead," I said, then immediately regretted it. "Poor choice of words."

"Helena—"

"I'm not leaving him, Henry." I didn't look up from my task of trying to get more water into William. "So you can either help or go away."

He was quiet for a long moment. Then he pulled up the second chair, settling into it with a sigh.

William let out a particularly vicious snarl, straining against the restraints hard enough to make the bed frame creak. I moved closer, pressing a fresh damp cloth to his forehead. Outside, night had fully fallen. Through the window stars were beginning to appear, bright and clear in the unpolluted sky.

"Grace would have known what to do," I said suddenly.

Henry's hand found mine, warm and solid. "Grace would have done exactly what you're doing. She would have stayed with him, refused to give up, driven everyone crazy with her stubbornness."

"You think so?"

"I know so." He squeezed my hand. "She learned from the best."

Around midnight, Begonia took over William-watching duties and Henry followed me downstairs. The house was quiet, most of the candles extinguished. Through the kitchen window I could see the courtyard, where the goats slept in piles and the braziers burned low.

"It's peaceful," I observed.

Henry leaned against the counter, studying me. "How long are you planning to do this?"

"Do what?"

"Sit with him. Refuse to sleep. Run yourself into the ground."

I turned to face him, crossing my arms. "As long as it takes."

"That's not an answer."

"It's the only answer I have." I turned to the window, pressing my palm against the cool glass.

Henry pushed away from the counter and came to stand beside me. He reached out, tucking a strand of hair behind my ear. The gesture was gentle, intimate, and it made my breath catch. "I'm with you," he said. "Whatever that means. However this plays out."

"Even if I'm wrong?" My voice came out barely above a whisper.

"Even then." His hand moved to cup my cheek, his thumb brushing away a tear I hadn't realized had fallen.

"That's possibly the most romantic and terrifying thing anyone has ever said to me."

"I have my moments."

I laughed. It was a small sound, broken and fragile, but it was real.

"Thank you," I said.

"For what?"

"For not thinking I'm crazy. Or for thinking I'm crazy and staying anyway."

"Oh, I definitely think you're crazy." He was smiling as he said it. "But you're my kind of crazy."

24

Tuesday

On the third day William began to calm down, as if resigned to his fate. I was running a cool, damp cloth over his still warm forehead when Begonia swept into the room.

"I brought brandy," she said, producing a bottle from the depths of her caftan like a magician. "For medicinal purposes."

"You're a saint."

"I am French. It is basically the same thing." She set the bottle on the desk and pulled out a second chair.

I nodded, too tired to argue.

"Is he getting better?" Begonia asked, her voice cautiously hopeful.

"Maybe," I said carefully, not wanting to jinx it. "Or maybe he's just tired."

But when I pressed the damp cloth to his lips, William's eyes focused on my face.

Really focused.

"William?" I whispered. "Can you hear me?"

He blinked once. Slowly. Deliberately.

"Oh my god," I breathed.

I leaned closer, searching William's face for any sign of the rage that had consumed him. "William, honey, it's Helena. Do you remember me?"

His lips moved. No sound came out at first, just a dry rasp. I held a cup to his mouth and he drank gratefully.

"Thirsty," he croaked.

I laughed, the sound half sob. "Yeah, buddy. I bet you are."

Henry appeared in the doorway. "Everything okay?"

"Maybe," I said, unable to keep the tremor out of my voice.

We spent the rest of the day monitoring William carefully, documenting every change. His fever began to drop. The redness faded from his eyes. By evening, he was asking for food.

"Can you bring him some broth?" I asked Begonia. "Something gentle on his stomach?"

"Of course, *mon cher*." She squeezed my shoulder before heading downstairs.

Henry moved to the bed, studying William with a critical eye. "How do you feel, kid?"

"Where's my mom?" William whispered. His voice was hoarse, damaged from days of screaming. "My tummy hurts."

Henry glanced at me. "Should we untie him?"

I hesitated, but nodded.

We worked together, loosening the sheets carefully. William didn't fight, just lay there watching us with those big dark eyes.

When the last restraint fell away, he immediately curled onto his side, pulling his knees to his chest.

"Thank you," he whispered.

My throat went tight. "You're welcome, honey."

Begonia returned with broth and we propped William up enough to eat. He managed a few sips before his eyes started to droop.

"Sleep," I told him gently. "We'll be right here."

But as I started to move away, his small hand shot out, grabbing my sleeve.

"Is my mom dead?" he whispered, his eyes filling with tears.

I settled back into the chair and took a deep breath. "I don't know," I forced past the lump in my throat.

William's eyes closed and he was quiet for a long moment. "Will you stay with me?" he finally asked.

I placed my hand over his, where it clutched my sleeve. "I'll stay," I said simply.

"Promise?"

"I promise."

His grip loosened slightly, but he didn't let go. Within minutes, he was asleep, his breathing deep and even for the first time in days.

I sat there in the gathering darkness and let myself cry.

***

The next morning, William woke up more himself. Still weak, still tired, but undeniably William.

"I'm hungry," he announced, his gruff little voice music to my ears.

"That's a good sign," I said, helping him sit up. "What sounds good?"

He thought about it seriously. "Pancakes."

"I'll see what I can do."

Begonia, bless her heart, produced the most gorgeous, fluffy pancakes I'd ever seen. William ate like he'd been starving, which, to be fair, he kind of had.

"Easy," I cautioned as he shoved another bite into his mouth. "You'll make yourself sick."

He swallowed and looked up at me, his expression suddenly serious. "Miss Helena?"

"Yeah, buddy?"

"Am I going to turn back into a monster?"

The question hit me like a physical blow. "No, honey. You weren't a monster. You were just sick."

"I was pretty scary though, wasn't I?" His lower lip trembled. "Mama always says I'm a handful when I'm not feeling well."

I had to bite the inside of my cheek to keep from losing it. "You were definitely a handful," I agreed gently. "But you're better now."

He was quiet for a moment, picking at his pancakes. When he spoke again, his voice was small. "Do you think Mama and Daddy left me because I was too naughty?"

Oh, fuck.

I set down the plate and pulled him into my lap, careful of his still-healing body. "William, listen to me. Your parents love you more than anything in the world. They would never, ever leave you because you were naughty."

"But they're gone," he whispered into my shoulder.

"I know, honey. I know." I held him tighter, this small, brave boy who'd been through more than any child should have to endure. "But that's not because of you. That's not your fault."

"Are they coming back?"

The question I'd been dreading.

I pulled back enough to look at his face. "I don't know," I said quietly. "I hope so. But even if they can't come back right now, you're not alone. You've got me, and Henry, and Begonia, and Rose, and Ashley and Jean Luc. We're all going to take care of you."

His arms tightened around my neck. "Promise?"

"I promise, buddy. You're stuck with us now."

He seemed to consider this, then nodded solemnly. "Okay. But I should probably warn you—I'm still going to be a handful sometimes."

"I would expect nothing less."

The door opened and Henry appeared with a tray. "Heard someone was hungry," he said, setting it on the desk. The distinctive aroma of steamed broccoli wafted toward the bed.

"Oh, no," William sighed, slapping a hand to his forehead.

A laugh bubbled up from my chest and I reached out to ruffle his curls.

He peeked out from between his fingers and began giggling, the sound bright and normal and so achingly precious that I had to close my eyes against the sudden sting of tears.

The bed shifted as Henry settled beside me and his hand covered mine. "You okay?" He asked quietly.

I opened my eyes to find both of them watching me with concern.

"Yeah," I said, my voice rough. "Yeah, I'm okay."

And for the first time in days, it wasn't entirely a lie.

25

Friday

William was chasing Bert the goat around the courtyard in circles while I sat on a bench, trying not to think too hard about several things, all at the same time.

"Penny for them?" Henry asked from his position by the makeshift fence, where he'd appointed himself permanent sentry.

"Just wondering if Robert is decomposing nicely at the bottom of Rose's Nazi well," I said conversationally.

One corner of Henry's mouth twitched up. "I assume so."

"You're not at all concerned?" I asked incredulously.

Henry cut his gaze to me. "I'm not intending to piss off Rose. Are you?"

"Absolutely not," I assured him.

"Then no, I'm not concerned."

Huh. Oh, well then.

I mean, I wasn't one hundred percent sure that Robert was dead. It was more like he'd never existed, which, given his sparkling personality, was probably for the best. And I honestly didn't care enough to investigate further.

William had finally caught Bert and was now attempting to convince the little goat to let him ride him like a horse. The goat seemed very uninterested in this offer.

I was considering getting up to intervene when the little boy suddenly veered in my direction. He climbed onto the bench, his small body warm against my side. Bert, who had followed him over, collapsed at our feet with what I could only describe as a dramatic sigh.

I pushed William's golden brown curls off his forehead. "You need a haircut."

"Are you sad?" he asked, ignoring me.

"A little," I admitted.

"Because of Miss Grace?"

My throat tightened. "Yeah, buddy. Because of Miss Grace."

He was quiet for a moment, swinging his legs and staring down at the little goat. "I'm sad about my mom and dad."

"I miss them, too."

"They might come back, you know," he told me, still looking down.

"Hey." I waited until he looked up at me and met his gaze. "Yes, they might come back," I said firmly.

William's little body sagged on a big sigh and he leaned his head against my arm. "Okay," he agreed quietly.

We sat there in silence as Bert pushed to his feet and wandered over to begin chomping on a potted plant. One of his compatriots knocked him away from the plant and Bert stumbled back into a bucket, which fell over with a clatter.

All four of the tiny goat's legs locked and he toppled over sideways.

"Goats are kind of stupid," William said with deep affection.

"Yeah," I agreed.

A shout rang out from the front of the house and we both jumped to our feet. Bert, who had just bounced back to his little hooves, fell over again.

"What was that?" William asked.

Another shout, the words rising up toward the end in excitement.

My hand automatically reached for William's shoulder as Henry came to join us.

"Let's go see," he said, leading the way into the house.

Inside, the lobby was empty and the front door stood wide open. Henry approached cautiously and froze in the doorway. I stood close behind him to take in the tableau at the front of the house.

Begonia and Jean Luc were running down the steps toward the gate, where an older man stood with a box in his hands. He was probably in his early seventies, lean and dapper, with round, metal-framed glasses.

And beside him—

"Mama!" William shrieked, wiggling his body between me and Henry, forcing his way out the door with surprising strength.

Jean Luc swept open the gate and pulled the older man into an awkward hug around his burden.

Darla darted past them, running toward the house. She was thinner and dirtier and had all new bruises, but the smile that split her face at William's cry was heartbreakingly familiar.

"William?" Her voice broke on his name.

The boy sprinted toward his mother with the single-minded determination of a heat-seeking missile. Darla dropped to her knees just in time to catch him, her arms wrapping around his small body as she buried her face in his curls.

The sound she made—half sob, half laugh, wholly grateful—made my eyes burn.

"You're okay," she was saying, over and over. "Oh god, you're okay, you're okay, you're okay—"

"I knew you would come back!" William's voice was muffled against her shoulder. "I knew it!"

Darla looked up, her eyes finding mine across the courtyard. Her face was streaked with tears and dirt and the kind of exhaustion that went bone-deep.

"Helena," she breathed.

I walked forward slowly, giving them space but unable to stay away. When I reached them, Darla stood, one hand still clutching William to her side, and threw her free arm around my neck.

"Thank you," she whispered fiercely into my shoulder. "Thank you, thank you, thank you—"

I couldn't force words past the lump in my throat so I just patted her back awkwardly.

"I was so scared," she murmured, the words just for me. "I couldn't remember—" Her voice cracked. "I didn't know if I'd—"

"You didn't," I said firmly, pulling back to look at her face. "He's okay."

"Because of you." Fresh tears spilled down her cheeks. "You kept him safe. You took care of my baby when I couldn't."

My throat was too tight for words, so I just pulled her back in, holding her and William together while they both cried.

Behind them, the older man cleared his throat delicately.

"*Pardonnez-moi*," he said, his French accent thick. "I do not mean to interrupt, but perhaps we should move inside? It is still not quite safe to stand in the open like this."

Henry had already moved to the gate, securing it behind them. "He's right. Let's get everyone inside."

He herded us toward the house, Darla refusing to let go of William even for a moment. I didn't blame her.

Jean Luc still had an arm slung over the older man's shoulder, his expression full of delight. "Henry, this is my friend Bertrand, from the village."

"Bertrand Mercier." He executed a small bow that would have been ridiculous if it hadn't been so charming. "I apologize for my previous lack of hospitality."

"How is the village?" Jean Luc asked. "When I saw you last—"

"Better," Bertrand interrupted. "Much better. Most have recovered." His expression softened. "Not all. But most."

"And those who wandered off?" Begonia asked from the doorway.

"We have been searching for them. Bringing them back." He gestured to Darla. "I found this beautiful young woman three kilometers from the village."

"I didn't know where I was," Darla said quietly. "I didn't know where William was—" She stopped, pressing her face into her son's hair.

"It's okay," William said, patting her arm with the comforting awkwardness of a child. "You were a bit of a handful, but I still love you."

"Thanks, buddy," Darla said with a watery laugh.

Bertrand had brought more than just Darla. He offered the box in his arms to Jean Luc, who accepted it with a sigh of appreciation.

"Potatoes," Bertrand announced proudly. "I thought you might need supplies."

"Potatoes!" Begonia clasped her hands together. "Oh, Bertrand, you beautiful man!"

She swept toward him, arms outstretched, clearly ready to bestow some very French thanks.

And that's when Rose appeared on the steps.

Bertrand froze mid-step, the potatoes forgotten. His eyes went wide behind his round-framed glasses.

"Rose," he breathed.

"Bertrand." Rose's voice was calm, but I caught the slight tremor underneath.

They stared at each other for a long moment. Then Bertrand pushed the potatoes into Jean Luc's arms and strode toward the steps.

Rose met him halfway.

He grabbed her face in both hands and kissed her.

He *kissed* her.

I stood there, mouth hanging open, as Bertrand tipped Rose backward and thoroughly demonstrated that age was just a number and passion was eternal.

"Oh, my god," Ashley whispered beside me.

When they finally came up for air, Rose was flushed and Bertrand was grinning like he'd won the lottery.

"I thought you were dead," Rose said softly.

"I am very much alive," he assured her. "Although after that kiss, I may need to sit down."

"So," I drawled slowly. "You two are—?"

"For the past twenty years," Rose said matter-of-factly. "Did you think I was celibate? I am old, not dead." She turned to Bertrand, her small hand cupping his weathered cheek. "I am glad you are safe, *mon étalon*."

"And I you, *ma cœur*." He kissed her again, more gently this time.

Begonia clapped her hands with a laugh. "Come, come! Everyone inside. We must celebrate this reunion properly. Let us put these potatoes to good use!"

In the kitchen, Darla collapsed into a chair. William immediately climbed into her lap and we shared a tired smile over his head.

"When did you last eat?" I asked.

"I don't think I have." She pressed her nose into William's soft curls. "It's all a blur. I don't have any idea what day it is or how long I was out there."

The little boy lifted his head and met her gaze with a frown. "It was a very long time. Don't do it again."

Darla pursed her lips but her eyes were twinkling. "Yes, sir."

William acknowledged her compliance with a firm little nod and laid his head back down.

Darla ran a hand over his back and met my gaze, shaking her head with a smile.

"That'll teach you," I told her, wagging a finger.

The afternoon was full of laughter that held a slight edge of hysterical relief. And potatoes. Lots and lots of potatoes. We washed and peeled half of Bertrand's bounty and Jean Luc sacrificed one of the older hens.

As a result, dinner was magnificent.

There were nine of us around the big table in the court-yard: three Americans, two Canadians, our three gracious hosts, and our new friend Bertrand, who proved to be a font of information.

"So the *gendarmes* just left again?" Henry asked incredulously between bites of hearty, well-seasoned stew.

Bertrand shrugged in the way that only the French can. "What more can they do, my friend?" He waved his fork, a piece of potato au gratin speared at the end. "They do not have enough men to leave one in each village. They said they will try to come at least once a week to check on us."

"Did they say anything about the electricity or the phones?" Henry probed. "Or tell you what's happening in the cities?"

"The landlines will be working soon, they say. Everything will be restored in time." Bertrand popped the potato into his mouth and swallowed before continuing. "The big hospital is open in Nice and the road is almost cleared. Those who need surgery are being taken there, but everyone else is to stay put for the moment. We are very lucky that Maurice recovered quickly and so far no one has had to be evacuated."

He leaned toward Rose with a raised eyebrow. "Gaspard was found naked in the fountain with a broken arm. The arm will heal but it was a death blow for his dignity."

"Oh, my," Begonia gasped before breaking into giggles.

When our laughter faded, Bertrand sat back in his chair and looked around the table. "I am afraid I have no news from outside of France, *mes amis.*"

I wasn't surprised and I tried not to be disappointed as the conversation moved on around me. As Begonia set a tray of fig tarts in the middle of the table, Darla leaned toward Ashley and asked about Robert.

Everyone froze.

Except for Rose, who stabbed a tart with her fork and dropped it onto her plate with a small smile. "Mr. Kovak had to leave us," she announced serenely. "We do not expect to see him again."

There were carefully blank faces all around the table. Henry caught my gaze and I shook my head, lifting my water glass to my mouth to take a sip.

"*Bon débarras*," Rose added.

I choked on my water.

26

Two Weeks Later

A little brown goat bleated at me in outrage as I body blocked him from coming through the kitchen door. It had been weeks since the day Begonia and I had herded the goats into the house in a panic but we were still trying to evict the opportunistic little beasts.

"No more goats in the house, buddy," I told him. Or her. "You've got the whole yard to play in again. Enjoy your freedom."

The goat yelled at me accusingly one more time and then trotted off to terrorize the garden. All of the villagers were accounted for and the authorities had declared the area safe, so Henry and Jean Luc had taken down the makeshift fencing around the courtyard and the goats were free to roam once more.

"You're welcome!" I yelled after the beast, pressing a hand to my lower back. Getting out of the shower this morning I'd taken a moment to admire my new muscles. Off-grid living was far more effective than any pilates class I'd ever taken, but every now and then my body reminded me I was, in fact, sixty-two years old.

Darla laughed from where she was watering the plants on the terrace. She was looking so much better these days. Her bruises were finally gone and the hollows in her cheeks had disappeared under Begonia's culinary care. "Are you arguing with the goats again?"

"He started it."

We'd fallen into an easy routine over the past weeks. Mornings with the goats, afternoons in the garden, evenings around the big table with too much wine and not enough answers about what was happening in the rest of the world. The French had restored the landlines across much of the country, but international lines and internet service were still down.

Grace would have been frustrated as hell.

"Have you seen Ashley this morning?" Darla asked, setting her empty bucket by the door. "We were going to go pick some more figs."

"I think she's in the library with Jean Luc," I observed. "He's helping her with her French. With the door closed."

Darla's smile was knowing. "Is that what we're calling it?"

"That's slightly more palatable than 'dusting the bottles', which is what Rose and Bertrand said they were doing in the wine cellar last night."

"Good for them."

We were still laughing when a rhythmic thumping cut through the morning air. The goats scattered, crashing to the ground in waves like dominoes.

"What the hell?" Darla grabbed my arm, her eyes wide.

The sound was unmistakable.

A helicopter.

"Inside," I said, moving backward and pulling her in behind me.

We ran for the front of the house and joined Henry, who was already standing at the window. He glanced over at me as I moved to his side, and I gripped his hand.

A large gray military helicopter appeared over the trees, sleek and official. My stomach dropped as it descended toward the courtyard, the downdraft sending dust swirling into the air.

There was a dark gray maple leaf painted on the tail.

"Oh, my god, it's the Canadians," I breathed.

Begonia burst from the kitchen, Rose and Bertrand close behind. Jean Luc emerged from the library with Ashley, both of them disheveled in a way that suggested I'd been right about the closed door. William appeared at the top of the stairs, rubbing his eyes.

"Mama?" His gruff little voice was still fuzzy from his nap.

"Everything's okay, baby." Darla met him at the bottom of the stairs and led him back to the window. He leaned into her side as she held him close.

Outside, the helicopter had touched down on the gravel, its rotors still spinning. The side door slid open and a figure in military uniform stepped out, holding a hand over his hat and ducking as he ran toward the house.

Henry opened the front door and we spilled out onto the tile as the officer approached. His gaze swept over each of us before landing on Darla.

"Mrs. Blackstone?" His voice carried over the whine of the engine.

Darla stepped forward, her hand still on William's shoulder. "Yes?"

"Major Thompson, Canadian Armed Forces. We've been searching for you." He turned back to the helicopter and waved his arm. "We're here to bring you home, ma'am."

William looked up at his mother, his eyes wide. "We can go home? Really?"

"Really." Major Thompson's stern expression melted into a soft smile.

Behind him, a figure appeared in the still open doorway of the helicopter. Tall and thin, the second man was dressed in casual fatigues, sporting bandages around his head and right arm. His left leg was in a walking cast. He extended a pair of crutches to the gravel and carefully swung his uncasted foot to the ground.

The officer standing in front of us shifted his gaze to me. "Mrs. Barrett?"

Busted.

"Major." I stepped forward, acutely aware that I was wearing mud-stained jeans and one of Eduard's old flannel shirts. I had an inch of gray at my roots and not a lick of makeup. I probably looked like a homeless person.

A well-spoken homeless person, but still.

"Ma'am, we have plenty of room on the chopper." He straightened slightly, military precision overriding surprise. His eyes swept over Henry and Ashley. "I'm authorized to bring back any other foreign nationals who wish to be evacuated. We're heading directly to the EU Central Command at Geilenkirchen. From there, we can arrange transport home."

The word exploded in the air like a grenade.

Home.

I opened my mouth to reply as Darla gasped beside me.

"Jacob?" She swayed and I instinctively reached out to steady her as my brain struggled to catch up.

Darla's gaze was locked on the man slowly limping his way toward us on crutches. Half of his face was obscured by bandages. The other half was scraped and swollen, the skin beneath the injuries was pale and had the faint yellowish-green shadows that linger after deep bruising.

Darla made a sound I'd never heard before—something between a gasp and a sob and a prayer all at once.

"It's Daddy!" William screamed, tearing away from his mother. "Daddy!"

"William, wait—" Darla started, but the boy was already running.

Jacob's crutches clattered to the gravel as he dropped to one knee and caught William. The impact nearly knocked

Jacob over backward, but he held on, his arms wrapping around his son with desperate strength.

"Hey, buddy," Jacob's voice was rough, thick with emotion. "Hey, I've got you. I've got you."

"You came back!" William was crying now, his small body shaking. "You came back!"

"I'm sorry it took so long." Jacob pressed his face into William's curls.

Darla had frozen halfway between us and them, her hands pressed to her mouth, tears streaming down her face. She took one step forward, then another, then she was running.

Jacob looked up just in time to catch her with his free arm as she collapsed beside them. The three of them tangled together on the ground, holding each other like they'd never let go.

"I thought you were dead," Darla was saying, over and over. "I thought I'd lost you, I thought—"

"I'm here." Jacob's voice cracked. "I'm right here. I'm so sorry. I'm so, so sorry."

Around me, everyone had gone still. Begonia was crying openly, her hands clasped to her chest. Rose had her arm around Bertrand's waist, her face uncharacteristically soft.

Ashley was pressed against Jean Luc's side, both of them watching with tears in their eyes.

Henry's hand found mine, squeezing gently.

Major Thompson cleared his throat delicately, giving the family a moment before approaching again. "That knee isn't meant to be on the ground, sir."

Jacob laughed, the sound watery but genuine. "Yeah, probably not." He accepted the major's help getting back to his feet—foot, really—and retrieved his crutches. Darla stood with him, one arm wrapped around his waist, William clinging to his other side.

"What happened?" Darla asked. "Dan—he attacked you. I thought—"

"Dan didn't make it," Jacob said quietly. "I almost didn't make it." He stopped, his jaw tightening. "They said it was close. Skull fracture, internal bleeding. But the medical staff in Nice, they—" His voice broke. "They saved me."

William pressed closer to his father's side, and Jacob's hand cradled his son's head.

Major Thompson lifted his chin pointedly. "We've been trying to evacuate Mr. Blackstone to the base for a thorough medical evaluation, but he refused to leave France until we found you two."

Darla nodded, not taking her eyes off Jacob. "How did you find us?"

The Major's gaze shifted to me. "We've been following up on any reports of foreigners among the survivors in the region. This place is past the edge of our search zone, but the locals said there was a large group of Americans." He turned back to Darla. "This is over ten kilometers from the accident site, Mrs. Blackstone."

Jacob lifted a hand to shift the hair falling across Darla's forehead, that partially covered the new scar there. "You walked here?" he asked.

"With broken ribs," I added helpfully.

Darla shrugged. "I didn't have a choice. And then I saw the sign and remembered this was where Helena was staying."

"That was incredibly lucky," Jacob said, turning to me. "I'm so glad you're okay as well, Helena. I never even dared to hope that you were all safe." He looked down into Darla's face, his eyes bright with unshed tears. "I didn't know if you'd been hurt in the accident or if you'd been infected as well."

Darla placed her hand on her husband's chest. "I was," she told him softly. "We both were. Helena saved us."

Confusion became horror on Jacob's face, which paled even further. He turned to me as tears began falling from his eyes and reached out a hand. I met him halfway and let him pull me in. "Thank you," he whispered hoarsely, his forehead against mine.

Now we were all crying. Great.

The Major cleared his throat. "Mrs. Blackstone? Mrs. Barrett? I can give you thirty minutes to gather your things. We need to get back to base before nightfall."

"Of course." My voice was steady. "Thank you, Major."

He nodded and retreated toward the helicopter, giving us privacy.

The silence that followed was deafening.

Darla looked at me and gave a watery laugh, her eyes full of tears. "I don't really have anything to pack," she admitted.

Begonia stepped forward, folding her arms around Darla and William gently. "Take at least a couple changes of clothes for both of you," she insisted. "And I will write down the number for our landline and you will call us and let us know you are safe, yes?"

Darla smiled. "Thank you," she whispered. "Thank you so much. William, stay with Daddy. I'll be right back."

"I don't want to go," Ashley announced as Darla slipped back into the house. Jean Luc stepped closer, his expression uncertain but hopeful.

"You could stay," he said quietly. "If you wanted."

She looked up at him, her eyes wide. "I could?"

"I know we have not known each other very long." The words came faster now, tumbling over each other in his nervous haste. "But these past weeks, getting to know you, I—" He stopped, switching to French, the words flowing more naturally. "*Tu es extraordinaire. Belle et gentille et—*"

Ashley launched herself at him, cutting off whatever else he was going to say with a kiss. When they finally came up for air, Ashley was crying. "Yes," she said. "Yes, I'll stay. I'll absolutely stay."

Jean Luc's smile could have lit up Paris.

Jacob looked between them, a bemused smile on his battered face. "So just you and Henry will be joining us, Helena?"

Begonia turned to me. "Is that what you want?" Her voice was flat, emotionless in a way I'd never heard from her before. Her eyes locked on mine, an unspoken accusation hanging between us.

"I don't know," I admitted. My voice came out smaller than I'd intended.

"Well, you have about twenty-five minutes to decide." Rose's voice was sharp as a blade.

"Rose—" Bertrand placed a gentle hand on her shoulder, but she shook him off.

I looked around the courtyard, taking in the honey-colored stone, the geraniums still clinging to life in their window boxes, and the ridiculous fainting goats scattered across the lawn like furry landmines. The faces of people who had become, against all odds, my family.

I looked at Jacob, who represented the best of what I'd left behind.

My throat was too tight for words.

"Helena." Begonia stepped forward, her hands grasping mine. Her rings were warm against my skin. "Please. Do not go."

"I don't want to go," I heard myself say.

The words surprised me as much as everyone else.

Henry's head snapped toward me. "What?"

"I don't want to go." The admission came easier the second time. "I don't want to go back to DC. Ever." I looked at Begonia, at Rose, at Jean Luc and Bertrand. "I want to stay here. With you. With all of you."

"Then stay," Rose said.

"It's not that simple."

Rose smiled. "Of course it is."

"You have told me there is nothing back there for you." Begonia's grip on my hands tightened. "You are not the First Lady anymore. You are just a woman named Helena. And Helena is welcome here for as long as she wishes to stay."

"Forever, if she wants," Rose added. "We have plenty of room."

"And plenty of wine," Bertrand contributed helpfully.

I laughed, the sound half sob. "We're all insane."

"Not insane," Rose corrected. "Just French."

I turned to find Henry watching me, his expression unreadable.

"What do you want?" I asked.

He was quiet for a long moment. Around us, everyone had the good grace to pretend they weren't listening with rapt attention.

"Helena," he said finally. "I kept my job to stay with you, and I quit my job to stay with you. I think it's clear where my priorities lie."

"That was different. It was only supposed to be a week."

"Was it? I never said that." One corner of his mouth quirked up. "I'm not leaving you, Helena. Period. No caveats. No deadlines."

"You're an idiot," I said, my voice rough.

"I try." He stepped closer, his hand finding mine. "For the record, I would very much like to stay. The wine is excellent and Rose hasn't shot me yet, so I'm calling it a win."

"I heard that," Rose called.

Henry ignored her, continuing, "But if you want to go to Germany or Washington or the Bermuda Triangle, I'm in."

Begonia let out a sound that was half laugh, half sob and pulled me into a crushing hug. "No Bermuda! You are staying here and that is that!"

"We're staying," I confirmed, my words muffled against her shoulder. "If you'll have us."

"If we will have you?" She pulled back, her eyes wet with tears. "Helena, you ridiculous woman. We love you. Of course we will have you."

"I love you too," I said, and was startled to realize how much I meant it.

A small voice cut through our moment. "Miss Helena?"

William looked up from where he was plastered to his father's side, his face crumpled with the kind of devastation only a six-year-old can manage. "You're not coming with us?"

Oh, hell.

I extricated myself from Begonia and knelt down on the gravel. My knees protested but I ignored them.

"No, buddy. I'm staying here."

His lower lip trembled dangerously. "But you promised you wouldn't leave me."

"You're going to leave me," I pointed out. "You're going home to Canada with your mom and dad, and you're going to be safe and happy." I brushed his golden brown curls from his forehead.

"But I want you to come too!" The tears started in earnest now, rolling down his cheeks. "You're my friend!"

"I will *always* be your friend." I pulled him into a hug. This small, fierce boy had wormed his way into my heart despite my best efforts. "Always. But friends don't have to be in the same place to care about each other."

"But how will I see you?"

"We will talk on the phone," I said firmly. "As soon as they get the internet working again, you can send me emails and we can make video calls."

He pulled back, considering this. "Every day?"

"Maybe not every single day," I smiled. "How about once a week?"

"Okay." He threw his arms around my neck again, squeezing tight. "Will you take care of Bert for me?"

"I will." I pressed my face into his curls, breathing in the scent of sunshine and goat and little boy.

Darla reappeared with a small bag, her own eyes red. "You're not coming with us, are you?" she asked knowingly as I pushed back up to my feet.

I shook my head and she pulled me into a hug. "I'll miss you so much."

"I'll miss you, too."

Jacob grasped my hand. "Call us if you need anything, Helena. Anything."

William pulled at the hem of my flannel shirt. "Will you wave when we take off?"

"I'll wave so hard my arm will fall off."

"Promise?"

"Promise."

Darla pulled me into another hug.

"Thank you," she whispered. "For everything."

"Take care of him," I said. "And of yourself."

"I will." She squeezed my shoulder once more, then they were boarding, ducking beneath the rotors. William pressed his face against the window, waving frantically.

I waved back, watching as the helicopter lifted off, climbing into the brilliant blue sky. We stood there long after it disappeared, the sound of the rotors fading into silence.

27

One Month Later

The courtyard of *La Maison des Fleurs* was transformed into a fairy tale. Rows of chairs had taken over the space with a narrow aisle down the center scattered with white rose petals. Above, the fairy lights were once again twinkling through the miracle of modern electricity, which I would never take for granted again.

At the end of the aisle stood a simple arch that Jean Luc and Henry had constructed from grape vines and lavender. The poor goats had been exiled to their shed all day after multiple attempts to chew on the decorations.

I stood near the back in a simple navy sheath that Begonia had grudgingly approved for the occasion and watched as the guests settled into their seats.

The entire village had turned out. Gaspard sat in the front row, his freshly healed arm no longer in its sling. The village doctor, Maurice, sat beside him in a surprisingly dapper suit, his yellow spandex nowhere in evidence. Bones had healed and bruises had faded, although the cheese man with his magnificent mustache gave Maurice a wide berth.

Henry appeared at my elbow, looking unfairly handsome in a dark suit. He'd found a barber in the village who'd tamed his hair into something resembling respectability, though I kind of missed the rumpled look.

"You clean up nice," I told him.

"I try." His eyes traveled over me, warm and appreciative. "You look beautiful."

Heat crept up my neck. "You're not so bad yourself."

His mouth quirked into that almost-smile I'd come to know so well as Ashley rushed up in a flutter of pale pink silk.

"Is everything ready?" she asked breathlessly. "The music, the flowers, the—oh god, did someone check on the cake?"

"Everything is ready," I assured her.

Jean Luc appeared behind her, wrapping an arm around her shoulders. "It is time," he announced with a smile.

Ashley laughed, her tension melting away. "I'm so excited!"

The crowd quieted as soft music began to play courtesy of the three piece ensemble that had taken up residence in the corner. Jean Luc offered Ashley his arm and they set off down the aisle.

Henry turned to me with a smile. "Ready?"

"Not in the least," I whispered, threading my arm through his and letting him lead me between the rows of chairs.

Begonia stood beaming at the end of the aisle, her celebrant's robes edged in silver and gold thread. As they approached her, Ashley released Jean Luc and they each turned away and took up positions on either side of the arch. Henry patted my hand before sliding his arm away and I turned toward Ashley, taking my place at her side. The five of us faced the packed audience as everyone turned in their seats to watch the bride and groom make their way down the aisle, hand in hand.

Bertrand adjusted his glasses and patted the white bloom in his lapel, but his eyes never left Rose. She was still tiny, but her square-necked gown of soft dove gray made her look like royalty. Her white hair was styled in soft finger waves, and she carried a simple bouquet of lavender and white roses.

And she was absolutely beaming.

They reached the front and stopped before Begonia who kissed each of them on the cheek before beginning the ceremony in French that flowed like poetry. I caught maybe half of it, but the important parts were universal.

Love. Commitment. Family.

When Begonia pronounced them man and wife, Bertrand swept Rose into a kiss that was entirely inappropriate for people their age.

It was perfect.

The courtyard erupted into applause and cheers. Goats bleated from the shed, the fairy lights twinkled. Begonia produced a lace handkerchief from somewhere and began to quietly sob.

Rose and Bertrand turned to face the audience and the cheers doubled. They began their walk back down the aisle and Henry offered me his hand. I took it, his fingers warm and solid and real as they laced through mine.

"They're brave," he said quietly as we followed the newlyweds.

"They're insane," I corrected. "Isn't it wonderful?"

His thumb rubbed over my knuckles, sending little sparks up my arm. "It is."

The reception was chaos in the best possible way. Wine flowed freely. Someone produced an accordion. There was dancing, the villagers spinning and laughing with the heady relief of survivors.

As the sun began to set, painting the sky in shades of pink and gold, Begonia appeared at the front of the crowd, her caftan billowing dramatically.

"*Mesdames et messieurs!* It is time for the bouquet!"

The unmarried women were herded into a group with varying degrees of enthusiasm. Ashley stood at the front, laughing at something Jean Luc whispered to her.

Rose turned her back to the crowd, her tiny frame radiating mischief. She counted down—"*Trois, deux, un!*"—and hurled the bouquet over her head with surprising force.

It sailed through the air in a perfect arc, spinning end over end, lavender petals scattering in its wake.

Ashley's hands shot up automatically, catching it against her chest. She looked down at the flowers in surprise, then up at Jean Luc, whose face flushed an adorable pink.

The party continued long into the night and I found myself on the periphery, watching it all with a wine glass in hand and something warm and unfamiliar in my chest.

It wasn't as bright and wild as joy. It was softer. Was it peace? It was more than that.

It was contentment.

"There you are."

I turned to find Henry approaching, loosening his tie. He'd ditched the jacket somewhere and rolled up his shirt sleeves. He looked more relaxed than I'd ever seen him.

"Here I am," I agreed.

"Dance with me?"

I let him take my hand, and we swayed there at the edge of the crowd.

"Hell of a day," Henry said, turning me in a gentle circle.

"Hell of a few months."

We danced in comfortable silence, and I let my head rest on his shoulder. My eyes slid closed and I didn't notice when the music began to fade.

Henry stopped dancing and I looked up. We'd moved away from the party and the lights. In the moonlight, his expression was soft, open, vulnerable in a way I'd rarely seen.

"Helena," he said quietly. "I need to tell you something."

My heart stuttered. "Uh oh."

"It's nothing bad. At least I hope not." He took both my hands in his, his thumbs moving against my palms. "I love you, Helena."

The world tilted slightly on its axis.

"I know it's complicated. You're still grieving. The world is a mess. This whole situation is insane. But I also know that life is short and unpredictable and I just wanted you to know." His hands tightened on mine. "I don't want to waste any more time pretending I don't feel what I feel."

I stared at him, my mind racing.

"You're an idiot," I said finally.

His expression flickered with uncertainty. "I've been told."

"I'm too old for this," I stated baldly. "I have gray roots and crow's feet and my knees crack when I stand up. I wake up at three in the morning to pee. I fall asleep reading. I'm a mess of grief and sarcasm and I don't even know who I am anymore—"

He kissed me.

It wasn't tentative or questioning. It was sure and steady and tasted like wine and promises and home.

When he pulled back, I was breathless.

"You are not too old," he said firmly. "And you are not a mess. You're strong, brilliant, funny, compassionate, and occasionally infuriating."

"Only occasionally?"

"Possibly frequently. But I love that about you, too."

I laughed at the absurdity of it all. "This is a terrible idea."

Henry smiled, his hands coming up to cup my face. "Is that a yes?"

"I didn't hear a question."

"Helena Barrett, will you marry me?"

I looked up at him—at his steady eyes, at the gray threading through his hair, at the lines that bracketed his mouth from years of almost-smiles.

"Yes," I whispered. "God help us both, yes."

He kissed me again, slower this time, sweeter. Behind us, the party continued, the sounds of celebration drifting across the gardens. Somewhere, a goat bleated. Someone laughed. Life went on, messy and beautiful and utterly unpredictable.

When we finally broke apart, I was smiling.

"So what now?" Henry asked.

"Now?" I linked my arm through his, turning back toward the lights and laughter. "We party."

"Now?" I linked my arm through his, turning back toward the lights and laughter. "We party."

More by Mary Jane Owen

Last Mom Standing

When Jane Kovak trades her cheating ex-husband and a cushy city life for an old Victorian farmhouse in the mountains of Virginia, she's prepared to face some challenges. Sulky teenager? Check. Leaky roof? No problem. Territorial chickens? Hmm, that wasn't in the real estate listing. A misogynistic neighbor with boundary issues? That's just great. A zombie apocalypse? Now wait a damn minute...

One day Jane is juggling her remote design job, single parenthood, and an assortment of quirky new neighbors. The next she's collecting stray kids and fighting off the infected with a hammer. Now the power is out, supplies are running low, and winter is setting in.

Fun times at the End Times.

Who says you can't have it all? In this warm, witty tale of family, survival, and a touch of romance, one woman proves that when the world ends, tough moms don't just survive—they thrive. Last Mom Standing is perfect for readers who like their end-of-the-world scenarios served with a side of humor and hope.

Available wherever books are sold.

https://amazon.com/dp/B0DT7QNR7D

Blast from the Past

Anne Welsh is a typical single mom...until she stumbles into a bank robbery and is outed as missing CIA agent Trixie Bigotti.

After thirteen peaceful years in suburbia, Trixie finds herself on the run with her teenage daughter. Between dodging aging mobsters and bumbling assassins, she has to come clean about her identity with the people who matter most.

FBI Agent Jay Stowe was madly in love with Trixie before her suspicious death and has carried a torch for her all of these years. When the love of his life pops back up—with a daughter who has his eyes—Jay is ALL IN.

It's time for this secret agent turned soccer mom to solve the mysteries of her past and protect her future from the dangers that surround her. Along the way she just may discover that she was never as alone as she thought she was.

Available wherever books are sold.

https://amazon.com/dp/B0B3S37QQT

What Goes Around

Trixie Bigotti is back and feeling good!

The bad guys are defeated and she's enjoying some quality time with a certain FBI Special Agent...

Codename: Hot Stuff.

It's been two months since Trixie put her past to bed and things are finally getting back to normal. She has a shiny new driver's license with her real name and she's not hiding from anything or anyone…except maybe commitment.

And men with machine guns.

Despite her best efforts, Trixie and the people she loves are once again at the center of a storm of trouble. The difference is, this time Trixie knows that she has help in her corner.

Trixie Bigotti may not be a secret agent anymore, but she's still got a few tricks up her sleeve. The bad guys who brought trouble to her little neck of the woods are about to have a serious case of regret.

Available wherever books are sold.

https://amazon.com/dp/B0DQYDRW8J

About the author

Mary Jane Owen is a pseudonym for Ms. Michael Owens, whose parents should never be allowed to name anything. An artist, teacher, single mother, and certified Crazy Dog Lady, Michael took an early retirement during the pandemic to write books in an old yellow farmhouse near the sea.

You can find more books by Michael at http://pepper backpress.com.

Want more?
@pepperbackpress

www.ingramcontent.com/pod-product-compliance
Lightning Source LLC
Chambersburg PA
CBHW051215190726

48288CB00006B/1974